"Hey, You—
The Boy at Stall Number Six!"

Nikki spun around to face the man striding toward her.

"What do you think you're doing?" he demanded.

His hand clamped on her shoulder. Lightning flashed through her mind. For a fleeting moment she wondered what it would be like to have that hand touching her in a caress.

He took a step backward, uttering a soft exclamation in French.

Nikki's cheeks colored. "Listen, if you've got something to say to me, speak English. If I'm to be insulted for my appearance, I want to understand it."

He threw back his head and laughed uproariously. "Pardon me, *mademoiselle,* I was just saying to myself, what a treasure of young womanhood beneath those grubby clothes. From the back, I mistook you for a boy."

Nikki met his look with a cool, level gaze. "And from the front?"

Dear Reader:

Nora Roberts, Tracy Sinclair, Jeanne Stephens, Carole Halston, Linda Howard. Are these authors familiar to you? We hope so, because they are just a few of our most popular authors who publish with Silhouette Special Edition each and every month. And the Special Edition list is changing to include new writers with fresh stories. It has been said that discovering a new author is like making a new friend. So during these next few months, be sure to look for books by Sandi Shane, Dorothy Glenn and other authors who have just written their first and second Special Editions, stories we hope you enjoy.

Choosing which Special Editions to publish each month is a pleasurable task, but not an easy one. We look for stories that are sophisticated, sensuous, touching, and great love stories, as well. These are the elements that make Silhouette Special Editions more romantic...and unique.

So we hope you'll find this Silhouette Special Edition just that—*Special*—and that the story finds a special place in your heart.

The Editors at Silhouette

SERL-7/85

PATTI BECKMAN
Odds Against Tomorrow

Silhouette Special Edition

Published by Silhouette Books New York

America's Publisher of Contemporary Romance

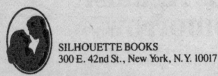

SILHOUETTE BOOKS
300 E. 42nd St., New York, N.Y. 10017

Copyright © 1985 by Patti Beckman

Distributed by Pocket Books

ISBN: 0-373-09270-9

First Silhouette Books printing October 1985

10 9 8 7 6 5 4 3 2 1

America's Publisher of Contemporary Romance

Printed in the U.S.A.

Books by Patti Beckman

Silhouette Romance

Captive Heart #8
The Beachcomber #37
Louisiana Lady #54
Angry Lover #72
Love's Treacherous Journey #96
Spotlight to Fame #124
Daring Encounter #154
Mermaid's Touch #179
Forbidden Affair #227
Time for Us #273
On Stage #348

Silhouette Special Edition

Bitter Victory #13
Tender Deception #61
Enchanted Surrender #85
Thunder at Dawn #109
Storm over the Everglades #169
Nashville Blues #212
The Movie #226
Odds Against Tomorrow #270

PATTI BECKMAN'S

interesting locales and spirited characters will thoroughly delight her reading audience. She lives with her husband, Charles, and their young daughter on the coast of Texas.

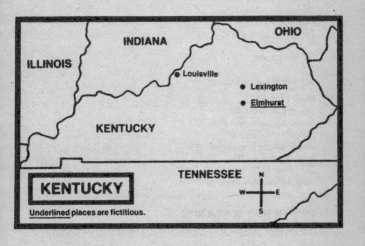

ILLINOIS

INDIANA

OHIO

● Louisville

● Lexington

● Elmhurst

KENTUCKY

TENNESSEE

KENTUCKY

Underlined places are fictitious.

Chapter One

No one in the mass of spectators at the track could possibly know how much it meant to Nikki Cameron to win this race.

At twenty minutes prior to post time on a lovely Florida day, nine jockeys filed into the sun-dappled paddock at Gulfstream Park, ready for the day's second race. Among the weather-beaten faces and diminutive bodies strode a stunning girl resplendent in colorful racing silks and highly polished riding boots.

Nikki Cameron was slightly taller than her compatriots, her slender five-foot-five frame dressed in cream-and-crimson riding colors. The bright outfit, though very expensive, was considered working clothes for a jockey. The cuffs of her black, over-the-calf boots were a cream color, which matched the tone of the riding pants and the triangles in the design of the silken top. On her right shoulder she wore the number three, indicating the post position of the horse, Spanish Lady, she had drawn for the race.

While the costume had the same male cut as the other jockeys, there was no mistaking the beautifully sculptured hundred and ten pounds of womanhood under the clinging silk. Her movements were those of the lithe, supple athlete that she was, capable of controlling half a ton of fiery thoroughbred in the mad plunge of a horse race.

Today, how well she controlled her mount would determine the course of her future. To the other jockeys it was a race to be won. To Nikki it was a step toward realizing the dream of her life.

In her left hand, Nikki carried her Caliente helmet, in her right hand a crop, the use of which she generally disdained. She squinted slightly against the brightness of the semitropical Florida sun, feeling its heat after the air-conditioned coolness of the quarters where the jockeys had been sequestered from weigh-in to the time their race was called.

The slight crinkle of her eyes gave some clue to the fact that she was in her mid-twenties. Aside from the minute lines that lent a note of enticing mystery to the large hazel eyes nested in long full lashes, she might have been a very desirable college girl who'd danced away the previous evening at a prom. Her lustrous dark auburn hair was sensibly pigtailed in two braids for the business of racing. When so much was at stake, there was no time to worry about being glamorous!

The fine film of perspiration on her rather high forehead was not entirely from the Florida heat. As she strode toward Spanish Lady, held in waiting for her by a groom, she was hardly conscious of the colorful foliage, the stately royal palms, the plumage of the birds— all the atmosphere for which Gulfstream was justly famous. She was in the grip of prerace tension. Her mind was totally occupied with the all-important minutes just ahead that would begin at the starting gate and finish either in or out of the money. Today, she *had* to earn her place in the winner's circle.

Her agent had contracted three races for her today in this meet. Bringing her mounts into the money could mean a considerable day's pay, despite the inroads of the agent's commission, expenses and the always hungry IRS. She had specific plans for the money. It would be added to the slowly growing amount that would one day make her dream come true. Realization of her goal dangled relentlessly in the future, but a win today could bring it a step closer.

She was barely aware of the rustle and jostle around her, the creak of saddle leather, the rise and fall of voices from the railbirds constituting the paddock crowd, the smell of horses and the dust underfoot. Computerlike, her mind was ticking off the characteristics of each horse and jockey who in a few minutes would risk life and limb in the pell-mell, thunderous effort to win. And she would be among them, riding her heart out for her dream.

Directly ahead of her in the paddock walk was Mershono, a gruff and shifty-eyed little jock who still resented a female jockey simply because his ego couldn't stand the thought of a girl beating him at the game he regarded as his domain.

Nikki thought that, thankfully, the Mershonos nowadays were becoming anachronistic. In no other field had women experienced quite this degree of difficulty crashing through the barriers. But having conquered every obstacle that could be thrown in their way, the female in riding silks couldn't be denied. At least not totally. Nikki was accepted almost completely. She had earned the respect of the track. Even the malingering male-chauvinist jockeys had to admit they had seen a professional ride after they had eaten the mud flung by the pounding hooves of the horse ahead with Nikki Cameron in the saddle.

None of them, however, knew the motivation that drove Nikki to make such a success of her profession. It forced her to ride a little harder, take greater risks, push herself and her horse to extra limits. That made her a deadly competitor. There was something about the fever burning in her eyes at the start of a race that gave more than one competing jockey a sobering chill.

The young woman in cream and crimson reached Spanish Lady's side. The filly was skittish, as if her racing plates were on hot sheet iron rather than the softness of the paddock ring. The great dark eyes were rolling. A bit of froth was at the meeting of bit bar and lip. Sotto voce, the groom was singing an old Spanish folk song to keep the nine hundred pounds of energy from exploding.

Ahead, Mershono dropped a sneering look over his shoulder as he draped two pairs of goggles about his neck.

It was a dry track, a perfect day for racing, thought Nikki—not like some of those gruelling battles with mud and grit flying up to sting and cake the face, blind the eyes, testing not only stamina and raw courage, but also a jock's adeptness at switching to clean goggles in the midst of a race. A wrong movement even in such a seemingly simple act could echo in a mount's rhythm and perhaps lose a race by a hundredth of a second. She was determined not to fall prey to such an error today. This race was too important.

Nikki started to exchange a smile to Mershono's sneer and decided that she wasn't being honest. He's really a little jerk, she thought, and impulsively gave vent to her true feelings. She stuck out the tip of a velvety pink tongue.

Among the gaggling, jostling paddock crowd was a fan who didn't miss the byplay. "Atta girl, Nikki!"

Mershono glowered in the direction of his heckler. Nikki dismissed the petty incident and focused her attention on the critical moments ahead. She felt a mild regret for the outcome of the drawing of lots in the racing secretary's office. She had drawn post position next to Mershono. He was riding Zero Gravity, a colt whose weight, nearly a hundred pounds more than that of Spanish Lady, belied his name. Those extra pounds might prove an enticement to a creep like Mershono to bump her on the break or going into the turn at the three-eighths pole.

She couldn't let that happen. She was on a carefully planned timetable that demanded a win today to bring her goal closer.

The mild trepidation was short-lived. Danger was part of the game. Jockeys did get killed. Scores were injured and maimed annually. This afternoon, in the clubhouse, she'd seen a once famous jockey now a paraplegic watching from his wheelchair. It was a fact of her profession that she had long ago accepted.

She knew that if she allowed the sour-tempered jockey, Mershono, to distract her too much, she was going to blow this contest of horseflesh. She couldn't let that happen. Not today.

"Riders up!"

The ancient clarion call from the paddock steward caused a faint catch of breath, an accelerated pulse beat in the hollow of Nikki's slender, lovely throat. It was always the same, this breath of heat across the skin, this nervous tension that would build up to the moment of waiting in the starting gate. Once the bell clanged and the gate flashed open, then the butterflies in her stomach would vanish, replaced by an icy calm, a kind of detachment, a total concentration on winning.

Meanwhile, she knew she must transmit none of the annoying jitters to Spanish Lady, already a bundle of screaming nerves.

Quickly she gave them all a final mental checklist, every mount, each rider. Ham Biscuit breaks fast, may tire, must not be permitted too much of a lead. Jesus Perito was on Circus Clown, a rail hog. Jimmy Simpson was riding Lil's Darling, a mean brute given to kicking grooms and biting jocks viciously if the unwary came within range.

Spanish Lady, her mount, was pure stamina despite her size. She had a compact back, which meant that her hind hooves, the driving pistons, would come down squarely below her center of gravity at each stride to hurtle her forward.

The journey from paddock to track was a measurement that could be taken in yards, but it always seemed hellishly long. Today, Nikki was hardly aware of movement as she dipped her Caliente-helmeted head a bit forward, her voice crooning softly to Spanish Lady while her fingertips touched the horse's withers reassuringly. Nikki felt the twitch of horseflesh. This time it had a slightly different quality. Nikki, experiencing the almost mystical rapport between horse and rider, sensed that Spanish Lady was steadying herself, preparing for the one thing she had been bred and trained to do, to run her heart out, to kill herself if necessary, striving to win the race.

For Nikki the sense of space and time had subtly shifted. She was surrounded by the racetrack ambience—the tension and excitement of the massed thousands in the grandstands, the blare of the loudspeaker, the bustling throngs pressing at pari-mutuel windows to get last minute bets down, the track aristocrats who purchased expensive clubhouse comfort to watch the race from the best vantage points while sipping tall, cool drinks.

The sea of sound presently wafting toward Nikki from the grandstand would become a roar when the race entered the homestretch, bringing shrieking bettors to their feet.

Nikki's sense of time was edged with a distended quality. Seconds became slow, drawn-out ticktocks. Her highly developed mental clock, capable of measuring a horse's space, speed, stamina, distances in fractions of a second, was poised and ready. Every nerve was as tight as a fine violin tuned to proper pitch just before the bow was drawn.

The two horses ahead were on the track, twisting, cantering in the first moments of preliminary warm-up.

Then, in a single, crashing instant, it all vanished.

Every thought of the race was wiped from her mind.

Like a powerful camera focused on the general scene, then zooming in with breathtaking speed to that one startling face in the crowd, her entire consciousness had been captured and frozen.

Later, she wondered what had caused her to turn and look directly into the clubhouse. Had it been the power of his gaze? Had it been that mysterious, unexplained human sixth sense of being stared at? Some kind of psychic witchery?

After all these years, did his eyes still have the magnetism to sweep aside known laws of time and distance?

There was no time to deal with the question. Nothing was real to her except the sudden, stunning impact of the man staring at her with such shattering intensity. She saw the burning dark eyes, the olive complexion, the high forehead, the curling black hair, the stubborn, masculine chin and curve of lips, and six years dissolved into a puff of smoke.

In that brief instant, across the distance, their gazes interlocked. Something like an unseen physical force struck Nikki a shaking blow. She gasped a name.

"Jacques Trenchard...."

No. It wasn't possible. Were her eyes playing tricks on her? Was this some kind of science-fiction time warp?

Had the tension of the race unsettled her mind? How could it be Jacques in this time and place?

Dimly she became aware of a beautiful red-haired woman standing beside him in the luxury of the club-house. She was speaking to him, but in that moment she might as well have been talking to a wall, so great was his concentration on the horse and jockey passing before him.

Spanish Lady sidled nervously, suddenly fighting the bit. Nikki's quick response, curbing the animal, was pure automatic reflex action.

Her heart was a lurching, pounding trip-hammer. She was trembling violently. A pain was tearing through her throat. Like burning torches, her eyes searched for a second, closer look. But the horses had moved on. The angle of her vision had changed. The handsome face, the dear lines around the mouth and eyes, the ridge of the jaw, the proud, arrogant tilt of the chin, all hated and loved for so many years, etched in her mind like an image burned there by a farrier's fire, were gone now, swallowed by the crowd.

A voice reached through her mental fog. It was the starter in the high stand overlooking the starter gate. "Number three! Spanish Lady. Get with it!"

Nikki's mind struggled desperately back to the job at hand. She turned her mount away from its moment of blind wandering, nosing the thoroughbred into the heavily padded number three stall.

"Good girl," Nikki murmured absently as the assistant starter closed the rear barrier, confining Spanish Lady and rider inside the boxlike stall.

Still going through the motions like an automaton, she slipped the protective goggles from the dangling position at her throat and seated them comfortably over her eyes. The familiar gesture helped her concentration return to the job at hand. But even as her senses awakened to her surroundings, the stirring of the powerful animal under her, the mingled, acrid smells of dust and horse sweat, her mind was filled with the question—had she actually seen Jacques? Would he lift his binoculars and center them on her throughout the race?

She desperately steeled her mind against the question, against anything connected with Jacques Trenchard and the flood of memories painfully buried, memories that she had just now discovered still had the frightening power to rise up and engulf her.

Stop it! she told herself sternly. Possibly it had not been Jacques at all. It might have been a trick played on her by a mind tensed and inflamed by the prerace jitters, an echo in the empty chamber so carefully built inside her heart, like a Pandora's box under lock and key. In any case, it didn't matter who was over there watching, Jacques or some stranger who bore a remarkable resemblance to him. You owe it to Spanish Lady, if not to yourself, for it not to matter! she chastised herself.

Fully in her element, Spanish Lady was an explosion as the starting gate sprung open. Nikki was dimly aware of the roar of the crowd and the thrilling cry of the racetrack—"They're off!"

Nikki was perched on knees bent to act as shock absorbers, body crouched from hips forward, spine straight. Her rider stance enhanced every wrench of horse muscle, every nuance of balance.

"She tends to break fast," the trainer had pointed out in the usual last-minute instructions. "Against this field, let her break as she will. She might well take an early lead, but keep in mind Diablo and Pageboy. Slower on the break, both of them, and in a sprint race you could take Lady out front all the way. But in this one..."

Nikki had listened, but anticipated every word, having ridden Spanish Lady twice before. The filly was out of a stable belonging to a successful movie star. Nikki had drawn her at Aqueduct, the big A, as well as at Keeneland when Spanish Lady ran as a three-year-old. Today, at a mile and a quarter, a total of ten furlongs, the horse that was built to sprint speed over the distance had to be reckoned with. The trick would be to clock the passing furlongs, judging the tick-tick-ticks of speed against Spanish Lady's stamina.

In the fury of the maelstrom, the thought of Mershono merely flicked through Nikki's mind. Spanish Lady was out and away before Mershono had a chance to get Zero Gravity in position for a challenge. Nikki had glimpsed Mershono's deadly serious face as she'd flashed past.

Her world dissolved into the thunder of pounding hooves. Wind and dust stung her face.

At the clubhouse turn, Spanish Lady was on the rail, leading by half a length. Diablo and Pageboy were still in the pack, not yet making a move.

At the five-furlong pole, with the backstretch straight ahead of her, the clock in Nikki's head buzzed a warning. *A little too fast.... Save a punch to match Page-boy and Diablo....*

Spanish Lady was straining to accept the challenge. "Not yet, girl! Steady...easy now...." Spanish Lady seemed to comprehend the meaning if not the actual words of the murmurings close to her speed-flattened ears.

Ham Biscuit had not made his usual blazing break and was lost in the pack. Circus Clown was moving up to challenge, as was Big Daddy.

Nikki was content to be running third as the leaders went into the far turn. Nothing yet from Diablo. Perhaps it was one of those days when, inexplicably, he failed to build to sprint speed. But there was Pageboy coming up on the right.

"He's the one, girl...the lathered black with the cherubic fellow riding...." Little Tommy "Buster" Brown, the jockey who, with his fair hair, freckles and baby-blue eyes, looked as if he should be sitting on his grandmother's knee reading from a storybook was cutting through the field of plunging racehorses like a scythe in quest of victory.

Nikki flicked assessment of Pageboy out of the corner of her eye. Buster was beginning to use the whip.

Nikki's brain computerized every clue of Spanish Lady's condition and situation. *Still third...every muscle moving perfectly, wind sound, spirit soaring, plenty yet in reserve....*

Nikki's mind flashed out the bottom line. *We're doing it, girl! Out of the turn now, down the home-stretch. We'll wrap it up....*

By inches, Spanish Lady was moving up. Pageboy was matching her stride for stride, but Nikki had the wild exhilaration of knowing that Pageboy's kick wouldn't quite match what Spanish Lady had in reserve. Nikki felt her heart swell with pride and love. For her, Spanish Lady was running one of the great races of her life.

Then, in the midst of all that sheer poetry of thoroughbred tendon and muscle, Spanish Lady suddenly flinched.

Sudden horror sheeted over Nikki as Spanish Lady jerked her muzzle up slightly. In an icy state, not time yet for outrage, Nikki realized that Buster Brown had also decided it was in the final analysis a two-horse race, his Pageboy against Nikki's Spanish Lady. He had further known which would be first and in the wildly straining, headlong pack, he'd leaned as if over Pageboy's neck and, with the hard butt of his crop, jabbed Spanish Lady in the stifle, that sensitive spot on a thoroughbred's upper hind legs just below the flank. Brown had assessed the nature of the hard-running pack as a rare opportunity to commit a foul that would probably be missed by even the strategically placed television cameras that viewed and recorded every yard of a horse race.

Brown's action served its purpose. For a split instant, Spanish Lady was off stride, fighting for balance, leaving Pageboy nosing out of the pack.

Nikki knew only too well what was happening and would happen in each minuscule grain of time. *The flinch...the stride breaking...balance teetering...the shattering contact of human leg against unyielding rail.... No pain yet, too much shock...the sudden panic erupting from Spanish Lady...the almost coldly objective assessive thought: We're going down to be trampled...horses tripping, falling, thrashing, their wild cries sullying the lovely Florida day....*

Broken thoughts. *My weight...all wrong in the saddle now. Spanish Lady must have a chance to recover...release....*

Nikki would never fully know whether her instinct had taken her off the horse or if she had been flung by jarring impact.

The blue Florida sky spun before her eyes. The huge tote board flashed across the sky. A wild thought: Where was Mershono of the gargoyllike face? She should have worried about the cherub....

Her last glimpse was of Spanish Lady, riderless, steady on her feet and running in the pack.

Then an explosive flash of fire inside her skull when her body, a projectile traveling forty miles an hour, struck the infield.

Instantly she was gathered into black nothingness.

Chapter Two

Nikki's senses stirred feebly. Dark emptiness ebbed to an awareness of cold gray mist, fog shredding itself in tendrils, struggling to admit light and sentience. It wasn't good. It was noisome, unpleasant. She wanted to draw away, but her pulsing force of life was insistent.

She felt no pain, only numbness. Her bodily parts seemed to have fallen away, leaving her nauseated. A light was bearing unpleasantly against the closed lids of her eyes.

Memory began to piece itself together, jigsaw pieces working into place. The bright sun at Gulfstream...the colorful paddock...the parade to the post through the ocean of sound rising from the grandstand. Jacques!

Yes, his face etched itself against the shimmering curtain of her returning mind.

Her eyes snapped open. Her lips were parted. She was breathing in short gasps.

Overhead was a ceiling of soft white. Sunlight washed gently between opened draperies, spilling over stark, impersonal furniture.

Hospital room...

Bits and pieces continued to fall into place. Now she remembered the sickening emptiness as she'd hurtled from Spanish Lady and the shock of impact. She had vague recollections of being on a stretcher and a ripping jolt of pain as she was placed in an ambulance. She remembered having a dreamlike thought, as if objectively viewing a stranger: They're taking me to a hospital because I've been injured.

The only consolation during the rush to the emergency room before anesthesia had blanked out her consciousness had been the thought that at least Spanish Lady hadn't gone down. Spanish Lady had escaped.

But now that wasn't consolation enough. With returning consciousness came a rush of bitter anger. She had lost the race and with it the purse that had meant so much to her. All on account of a crooked little weasel of a jockey named Buster Brown. She felt the primitive fury to kill.

"Welcome back," said a gruff female voice at her side.

Nikki painfully moved her head a few inches. Standing beside the bed, smiling reassuringly at her, was a large woman in a nurse's uniform. Her freckles and ruddy complexion were evidence that the gray hair tucked under her nurse's cap had once been red. Piercing blue eyes glittered behind horn-rimmed glasses.

"I'm Mrs. McGuire," she introduced in a voice that would have placed her at the bass end of a ladies' barbershop quartet. With surprising gentleness for a woman of such Wagnerian proportions, she wound a blood pressure cuff around Nikki's arm, pumped it up and adjusted a stethoscope to her ears.

Nikki was becoming more aware of her surroundings as feeling returned with uncomfortable needle pricks. She realized that her left leg was encased in a cast and hoisted in traction. Her shoulder was beginning to throb. There was a cramping in her back. Her hair was in tangles. For just an instant her eyes stung with tears of despair. No, this simply couldn't have happened to her. Not now. Not when so much was at stake. Banshee! The Kentucky Derby!

She struggled up on an elbow.

"Hey, hold it, kiddo!" Mrs. McGuire planted a broad hand firmly on a shoulder and pushed Nikki back into the pillows. "You're not going anywhere!"

"You don't understand!" Nikki cried. "I can't be lying around here. I have to get back to Elmhurst. My horse, Banshee. I have to ride him—"

"With a cast on your leg?" The buxom nurse chuckled. "I'd pay money to see that."

Nikki stared up at her helplessly. How could she make her understand? All of her plans—her dream—swept away in an instant by this rotten stroke of bad luck.

"How bad is my leg?" she demanded. "How long am I going to be laid up?"

"Well, you're going to have to ask the doctor those questions, dear." The nurse finished her ritual with the blood-pressure instrument and patted Nikki's arm, her eyes softening with a sudden look of compassion. "Feelin' kind of rough, huh?"

"You bet," Nikki mumbled.

"The doctor left orders for something to ease the discomfort...."

"Maybe later, if it gets worse. I hate this groggy feeling as much as anything else."

"Well, that's the effect of the anesthesia and Demerol. It'll wear off."

Nikki touched her tongue to her dry lips.

"Here," the large woman said with a nurse's instinct. She held a glass a water with a plastic straw to Nikki's lips. Gratefully, Nikki took several swallows of the cold liquid. Then she asked again, "How badly am I injured?"

"Not too much, considering the fall you took, kiddo. You must be made out of tough material."

Again Nikki felt foolishly close to crying. "My leg..."

"The doctor will be by in a little while and answer all your questions," Mrs. McGuire hedged evasively, straightening the pillow. "Meanwhile, you have some visitors, if you feel up to it."

"Visitors?"

Why did the image of Jacques Trenchard instantly wrench across her mind?

"W–who—?"

"Well, the gentleman says he's your father—"

"Dad!"

"—and he has a youngster with him—"

"Johnny!"

"Hey, whoa." Once again the nurse pushed her firmly down. "None of that rearing up on your elbow or Dr. Masters will hang a 'No Visitors' sign on your door and me with it!"

Mrs. McGuire's crêpe soles rustled their way across the tile floor. The door closed behind her, then, in another moment, was pushed open by a broad-shouldered man whose deeply tanned features were accented by a shock of steel-gray hair. Close beside him, looking uncertain and tearful, was her son. Johnny gulped and said bravely, "Hi, Mom."

From the scrubbed look of his snub-nosed face, Nikki knew tear stains had been washed away. Her father had gently steeled the boy in the aftermath of the disastrous news. And for an instant, Johnny was very manly standing there.

Through a blur of her own tears, Nikki drank in the sight of her son's curly, jet-black hair, olive complexion and beautiful huge, dark eyes fringed with thick lashes. She saw the youthful mirror image of his father, Jacques Trenchard....

Again the face in the crowd flashed across her mind with searing intensity.

A sudden cry broke from Johnny's throat. "Oh, Mom!" He flung himself toward the bed before Colby Cameron could grasp his hand. Childlike, his overpowering impulse was to throw himself into his mother's arms. But he caught himself at the last instant, drawing up at the bedside, wiping his palms uncertainly on his jeans. Tears welled in his large eyes. He gulped and said, "Gee, you've got a shiner like that time I fell out of the tree."

Nikki laughed in spite of the ache it brought to her bruised ribs. "Come here, honey." She held an arm out and Johnny buried his face in the hollow of his mother's neck. She comforted him as the tears he could no longer hold back spilled from his eyes. "It's all right, sweetheart. Mommie's going to be fine."

She turned her head, looking up at her father. He came to her, bent and touched her forehead with a gentle kiss. Then he managed his broad Cameron smile. "You look like hell."

"Guess I do. I feel that way, too. In more ways than one."

"But you're beautiful. Isn't she, Johnny?"

The boy nodded.

"How did you get here so quickly?" Nikki asked.

"Well, we got a phone call a few minutes after it happened," Colby Cameron said. He ran lean fingers through his mane of steel-gray hair. "It so happened Chumbly was at Elmhurst in his private jet."

Chumbly, Nikki knew, was the sixth earl of Kenilshire, Richard Cummerson. Colby had told her Chumbly could trace his lineage back to the time when Newmarket, in England, was a thinly populated area. That location started on its way to renown in the racing world when King James saw it as a sporting center and his grandson, Charles II, build a small palace on the site in the 1660s, bringing his court to witness the gallops of Warren Hill. The Cummerson thoroughbred tradition had begun in those days and had continued unbroken to the present.

"Chumbly," Colby went on, "was at Elmhurst on one of his annual jaunts to the States to sip tea with

British gentility while horse-trading like a pirate. He made a pitch for Banshee.''

A cold sensation flashed through Nikki. The nurse's stern command was forgotten. She raised herself on an elbow, her eyes blazing. ''I hope you told him no!''

''Hey, take it easy, honey. You know I wouldn't sell your horse.''

Nikki sank back. At least she was relieved on that score.

''Anyway, the minute we got word about your spill, Chumbly had his pilot rev up the Lear and we buckled in and flew down without even taking time to grab a toothbrush.''

''We didn't have time to get you any flowers, Mom,'' Johnny apologized.

''You're all the flowers I need, big fellow.'' Nikki's palm caressed the smooth cheek that would someday grow a blue-black stubble. Like his father. The thought came with a strange, inner wrenching sensation.

Looking up at her father, she asked, ''Have you talked with the doctor? I want to know what is broken and how long it will take to mend. I can't get that nurse to tell me anything.''

''Mrs. McGuire? Boy, she's something, isn't she? I keep visualizing her carrying a shield and a spear in *Die Walküre*. But, yeah, I talked with the doctor. You had a mild concussion, multiple bruises, a cracked rib and a slight lateral facture of the biped, which is the reason for the cast.''

''Slight? And they harness me in this rig?''

Her father shrugged. "Probably to keep the tendons stretched behind the damage and keep you off horses for a while."

A coldness pricked her heart. "How long a while? Dad, you know I can't be laid up—not now of all times!"

He reassured her, "Long enough to revise our schedule but not upset it irreparably." The corners of his eyes crinkled. He teased, "If you had to break a leg, you were considerate enough to do it at the outset of the three-year-old season. Plenty of time now between the month of May and Churchill Downs. Little Willy Farlow will do nicely on Banshee during the early prep races."

Prep races—important stakes and handicap races, really, races that many stables would be proud and content to win. But they were races that would winnow out all but the champions for that ultimate race, that two minutes of running in a race at the Downs known simply as the Kentucky Derby. And her Banshee was going to run in that race. She had willed it so.

"So when do I get out of here?"

"Don't go chafing at the bit like a Cameron," he ordered. "They'll give you the boot soon enough. Then we'll whisk you out to a plane at Miami International and back to Elmhurst before you've really had a chance to enjoy this lollygagging."

She sighed. "I don't seem to have much choice."

"None whatever." Her father gave her a narrow-eyed look. "What happened on that track, anyway? You're too good a rider to just run into the rail like that."

"It was no accident," she said through her teeth.

"You were fouled, right? I figured as much. Why didn't the stewards catch it? Were they all blind?"

She shook her head. "He picked the right spot. We were all bunched together. I doubt if the cameras caught it."

A scowl crept across Colby's face. His blue eyes turned cold and hard. "Who was it, Nikki?"

She looked at the cold fury in his eyes. She knew the low boiling point of his Irish temper. Her gaze moved to his big, scarred hands. In his day, he could more than hold his own in a barroom brawl. Right now he was a match for most men half his age. More than a match for a pint-sized jockey.

Her lips moved in a wry, sad smile. She shook her head. "I'm not going to tell you."

"I can sure as hell find out. By now I'm sure there are people who know even if the judges don't have proof."

She reached for one of the big, strong hands. "No, Dad," she said softly. "We have enough of a problem on our hands. I need you now like I've never needed you before if I'm going to get Banshee to the Derby. I can't make it without you, which I'd have to do if you were sitting in jail for breaking a two-bit jockey's neck. Wait until after the Derby and I'll do it myself."

Colby's face split into a wide grin as some of the anger relaxed. "You could probably do it, too!"

She gave a sigh of resignation. "I'll just have to live with this somehow, and be thankful it wasn't worse." Then she smiled at her son. "Johnny..." She patted the narrow empty space beside her. "Guess we might as well make the best of a bad situation. Why don't you crawl up here beside me, stretch out and make yourself comfortable. We'll turn on the TV set."

"Well...if you think it's okay," he answered uncertainly.

"Sure it is. We can play like we're in the den at home. I'm half snoozing in the big reclining chair and you're on your back on the carpet with the big red pillow propping your head when *Sesame Street* comes on."

"Okay." He grinned. He eased up beside Nikki, very cautiously and carefully.

"There," she said. "You see? It's like having a little robin redbreast slip down beside me and say 'Hi' and keep me company."

Colby Cameron looked down fondly at his daughter and grandson. "Since there isn't a horse race on the tube right now, I think I'll go find out if the coffee here is as bad as it is in most hospitals."

He left, and shortly thereafter Nurse McGuire came in. She scowled at Johnny. "We already bent the rules, allowing a child in your room—"

Nikki, feeling stronger by the minute, scowled back, her hazel eyes flashing defiance.

There was a silent moment, a testing of wills. Then Mrs. McGuire grumbled, "Next I guess you'll be wanting dinner for two served in here."

"Where else would Johnny and I dine this evening?"

The large nurse stood there a moment longer, engaged in a silent struggle between her dedication to hospital rules and her nurse's fierce instinct for what was best for her patient's morale. Finally, muttering to herself, she turned and walked out.

Nikki and Johnny looked at each other like two conspirators who had just gotten away with playing hooky and broke into giggles. Johnny wriggled slightly, bunching the pillow a little higher behind his head. The faint movement brought a catch of pain through Nikki's shoulder, but she thrust it aside. Having his precious little-boy presence near her was a tonic no pharmacist could concoct. They settled down to watch a rerun of "Batman."

The interlude passed too quickly. Big, brusque Dr. Masters came in, charts in hand, to tell her things were looking good for her and remark on her luck in not having gone down in a pile of screaming horses. He assured her that she would be able to leave the hospital soon and return home to convalesce. The nurse was in and out. Dinner came and went. Her father returned wanting to know if there was anything she needed or wanted that he could go and fetch.

Then they were framed in the doorway, the love in their voices warming her as they told her good night. They turned to leave, the stalwart man holding the little boy's hand.

Moving away, the boy turned his head to stretch out his parting look at her as long as possible.

"Don't forget your prayers, Johnny."

"I won't." He grinned. "Sleep tight; don't let the bedbugs bite."

Then she was alone in the emptiness of the room looking at the vacant doorway, holding on to the image of his sweet young face.

The next day a large bouquet of roses was delivered to her room. With it was a white card. In one corner, embossed in gold, was a familiar family crest. On the card was a single scribbled name.

"Jacques."

Now she knew the face in the crowd at the race-track had been no figment of her imagination. He was here, in the United States.

Chapter Three

The familiar ambience and busy hours of Elmhurst welcomed Nikki home from the hospital. She would be forced to hobble around with the cast on her leg for a few more weeks, but at least it was a welcome change from the harness in the hospital bed.

Elmhurst. Nikki thought the name was almost synonymous with heaven. With six white columns fronting a shaded veranda, the stately old colonial mansion was set on a low promontory that offered a vista of lush green pastures and meadows broken by hoary, ivy-grown stone walls and majestic trees that turned from deep green to startling crimson and gold at the first nip of autumn frost. Rustic footbridges traversed a gurgling creek that was banked by moss, laurel and rhododendron. Lined with lovely elms, the white-graveled driveway wended its way from an old wrought-iron gate set between two ancient stone pillars at the highway. The cosmopolitan city of Lexington, flavored by the internationalism of the thoroughbred world, was a short drive northward.

The bursting vigor of life never paused at Elmhurst. Weanlings cavorted in fields of succulent grasses with the sheer joy of being alive. Proud mares and stallions romped over their domain as if conscious of their royal status. Two-year-olds worked out exuberantly at the training track in the atmosphere of champions.

North of the main house were the barns with their rows of stalls facing wide, shaded concourses that cut a geometric pattern of white against the green of the countryside. Dotting the landscape in the vicinity of the main house were the weathered brick homes of most of the Elmhurst population: grooms, stable boys, trainers, veterinarians, field hands and agronomists. There was a tall white silo, a squat old hewn-log smokehouse, garages for cars, tractors, plows and cultivators and a smith. A catch-all toolshed rounded out the built-up environment of an enclave almost feudal in its capacity to attend to its own needs. There was even a back-up generator to provide power in case a failure of the public electric utility created a brief emergency.

When Colby brought Nikki home from the airport, Elvira Ledbetter, the spunky octogenarian who had hired Nikki's father to raise and train her million-dollar string of horses, was the first to greet her. Elvira was a silvery little wisp who walked with a cane but had the temper and fire to whack knuckles with it if aroused.

Nikki was settled in a reclining chair in her comfortable bedroom. Great windows afforded a second-story view of the rolling Kentucky bluegrass pastureland crisscrossed with white fences. She remembered how excited and filled with optimism she had been when she'd left Elmhurst for the race at Gulfstream. Now she had come back in defeat, depressed by losing the race and by her injuries. Adding to the mental turmoil had been the unsettling shock of seeing Jacques Trenchard and feeling once again all the violent emotions he could stir in her.

Johnny was beside her, rattling on about the latest colt foaled in the stables, but he fell respectfully silent when Elvira rapped on the door with her cane, then bustled in.

"Dirty shame what happened to you, child," Elvira stormed, banging the floor with the tip of her cane, her sharp, black eyes flashing like sparked coals.

Nikki agreed with a wry smile.

"Colby tells me you were fouled by another jockey. You're going to bring charges, of course?"

"Oh, what's the use, Elvira?" Nikki sighed. "At first I was mad enough to do just that. But I've had time to cool off and be more realistic about the situation. The cameras didn't pick it up. It would be my word against his. You know what everyone would say, that I made up the story to cover my own bungling ride."

"Everybody," Elvira countered, sitting on the edge of a cane-back chair facing Nikki, "already knows damn good and well what happened!"

"Yes, the people who count know. And that's what matters to me. Right now, Elvira, I'm just thankful

Spanish Lady didn't wind up with a broken leg and I didn't wind up dead. It's not the first time I've gotten hurt falling off a horse.''

"Well, it's your decision," the elderly woman muttered, rapping the floor with her cane for emphasis. "You can bet I wouldn't let him off the hook that easy."

"Don't worry," Nikki muttered through her teeth, "it's a personal score I'll settle one day."

"Knowing you, I wouldn't be surprised." Then she patted Nikki's hand. "You're right to be thankful it wasn't worse than it was. I had you in my prayers, child."

"I know, Elvira." Nikki smiled, her eyes misting with a wave of affection for the older woman. Elvira was more to her than mistress of Elmhurst and her father's employer. She had become like a grandmother after Nikki, then a rebellious teenager, had come here to live after her real grandfather and her mother had died. She'd grown to love Elvira so much she'd wanted to call her "Grandmother," to which Elvira had responded with an indignant snort, "You want to make me feel like an old woman? You call me 'Elvira,' young woman, you hear?" Nikki had never made *that* mistake again.

"Now then, you've got another visitor," Elvira said, rising from her chair. "I hope you're not too tired to say hello to Orlis. That darn fool has been pestering me all day, wanting to know what time you were getting here."

Nikki felt another tug at her heart. Along with her father, Elvira and her son, Johnny, Orlis Washington was an integral member of her family cluster. Now chief groom, Orlis kept Elmhurst stables functioning with a quiet managerial skill and unsurpassed comprehension

of thoroughbreds. But his place in Nikki's life pre-
dated Elmhurst, all the way back to her earliest memories when he had worked for her grandfather in her
childhood home, Crestland. It was Orlis who had given
her her first riding lessons, putting her on a pony almost as soon as she could walk, teaching her the intri-
cacies of thoroughbred handling as she grew up.

"Yes, I do want to see Orlis." She smiled.

"Sure you're not too tired?"

"Of course not. I'm fine, Elvira. The only thing that
I got tired of was lying around in that hospital bed."

"Well, I'll send Orlis up, then."

Elvira left and in a few minutes there was a tap at her
door. "Come in, Orlis," Nikki called.

Orlis Washington was a lean, sinewy man. Nikki had
no idea what his age was. Exept for a sprinkling of
white in his hair, he looked no different from the Orlis
who had put her on her first pony.

She held out her hands and Orlis gravely squeezed
them. "It's good to have you back, Nikki." The digni-
fied reserve in his voice was contrasted by the glowing
warmth of his eyes. "We were all worried about you."

"Well, I'm doing just fine now, Orlis, except for this
stupid cast I have to wear a few more weeks."

"I was telling Mom about the new foal," Johnny
piped up.

Orlis smiled. "Yeah, you ought to see that one,
Nikki. He's got the look of a sure winner."

"I can hardly wait to get down to the stables." Then
she asked the question that was burning her lips. "Tell
me about Banshee. How is he?"

Orlis chuckled. "Rambunctious as usual. I swear that horse has been missing you. He's been restless and cantankerous ever since you've been gone. I'll bet he quiets down the minute you walk in the stable."

"I'm dying to ride him again—" Her voice halted as she looked ruefully at her cast. "I guess that will have to wait for a while. I'll be doing fine if I can just hobble down to the stables."

"Yeah, we've been talking about that. We knew you'd want to get all over the place, so we've rigged up a golf cart. Got it waiting downstairs, batteries charged and ready to go."

"Hey, that's a brilliant idea!" Nikki exlaimed, suddenly filled with excitement. "I can get out to the training track, the pastures..."

Orlis said, "Well, I've got to get back to the stables. Just wanted to tell you I'm glad you're back."

"Thank you, Orlis."

Their eyes met for a moment in silent communication. Nikki thought of the years he had shared with her, the times of her happy childhood, the thrill of her first rides, the joy and warmth that had been Crestland, her real home, the tragedy they had lived through when the land was taken away from them and the turmoil Jacques Trenchard had brought to her life.

Jacques. His name springing into her mind started little trip-hammers banging at her temples. He had scarcely been out of her thoughts since that day at the racetrack in Florida. She remembered the shock of his flowers and card. Her emotions had gone into a tailspin. Would he come to the hospital? Anger flared in her, battling with the bittersweet heartache of remembering other days and nights. Heat suffused her body at the thought of those nights.

Fury whipped through her. Would she never be rid of the ghosts?

No, he had not put in an appearance at the hospital. She had relegated the whole incident to its proper perspective. A chance encounter. He had been at the tracks with his latest conquest in tow. Nikki had placed her. The red-haired Italian movie actress, Gina Anotia, was linked romantically to Jacques in recent newspaper and tabloid stories. The flowers had been a gesture. It was second nature for him to make the gallant gesture under such a circumstance. By now he was back in Europe, no doubt, at Monte Carlo, the Riviera, or his family estate, with no more thought of the stormy episode in his life that involved Nikki.

Looking at her son, Johnny, she felt a wave of relief. And yet the disturbed emotions stirred by seeing Jacques lingered on. She was eager to get busy again, to get her mind on other matters, to occupy her thoughts with Banshee and the ride to glory that could change all their lives and make her greatest dream come true.

Early the next morning, Nikki hobbled downstairs with the aid of her crutch and found the golf cart Orlis had described. She was delighted to have the mobility to ramble over to the stables, the pens, the pastures of Elmhurst.

For most of Elmhurst, the day began at the first glint of the sun. Stalls were cleaned; horses were fed the carefully supervised diets of grain and added nutrients—four feedings daily for in-stable horses. Expert hands gave first grooming, noting conditioning, taking care of a pulled tendon, a tenderness in the frog of a hoof. Horses were exercised, cooled and given a full grooming.

Meanwhile, the routine of running a multimillion-dollar enterprise was smoothly clicking. A van arrived with a brood mare for a studding by an Elmhurst stallion. A luxury car pulled in the winding drive or a private jet touched down at the Elmhurst airstrip bringing an oil-rich Texan or Arab or newly famous entertainment star to bargain for an Elmhurst two-year-old or stud.

This was Nikki Cameron's world, the milieu soaked into every fiber of her being. She enjoyed every moment of it. She simply loved thoroughbreds, their spirit and fire, their sensitivity and their loyalty and inherent proclivity to reach out in total unselfishness to a human being who would respond.

Johnny was up bright and early, eager to ride with her in her golf cart. "Where are we goin' first?" he asked, bouncing on the seat with restless young energy.

"Now where do you think?" Nikki grinned.

"I bet I know. To the stables to see Banshee."

"Well, you just won the bet!"

They had barely trundled away from the main house on the golf cart when Clem Smathers, the farrier, spotted her and came running up to her on long, lanky legs.

"Miss Nikki! Welcome home."

"Hello, Clem. Nice to be here."

"You're lookin' fit."

"Thanks. You should have seen me after they picked me up out of the Florida dirt!"

Clem looked nothing like a village smithy. He was young, tall, skinny. With his lanky brown hair and straggling mustache he resembled a throwback to a hippie commune of the sixties. But at a forge, those incredibly long arms could do more with a hammer, tongs and white-hot iron than any other in the state.

He said, "Hi, Johnny."

"Mornin', Mr. Smathers."

The farrier nodded at the vehicle. "I see Orlis got you fixed up okay with the golf cart."

"Yes, it's really a neat idea. Beats hobbling all over the place with a crutch."

"Well, you got back at just the right time."

"What do you mean?"

"Banshee. He's got a loose shoe. I spent a sleepless night wondering how we were going to handle it. I guess I live right—pay the preacher on time—because here's the answer to my prayers: Miss Nikki to the rescue."

Nikki knew that Clem was the toughest of farriers, fazed at nothing horses did, except in the case of Banshee. Thoroughbreds have a bottomless bag of quirks. And Banshee had long ago decided, for no fathomable reason, that he wasn't going to be shod. He could turn into a hurricane of kicking, squealing, rearing, biting fury. One way or another, Clem would get the job done. But Nikki could make it easier for everyone involved. They had discovered this one day while the stallion was raising the roof at being shod. Nikki had raced into the smithy to ask the horse what was going on and wasn't he ashamed of himself. Another unforeseeable quirk had surfaced in the big fellow. He would submit to the shoeing as long as Nikki stood with an arm draped across his arched neck and petted and cooed and scratched and murmured in his ear that he was the greatest, the most beautiful horse in all the world. He stood, whinnying softly and gobbling up the attention like a finger-sucking weanling. If there had been any question before, after that day every hand at Elmhurst recognized the special bond between Nikki and Banshee.

"I'm just dying to see that big, beautiful monster," Nikki exclaimed.

"Well, here he comes now."

Nikki turned. From the stables appeared a great black stallion with white stocking legs and a white star on his forehead. His sleek hide gleamed in the sunlight. "Banshee!" Nikki exclaimed.

She felt her breath catch in her throat. She never failed to feel a surge of adrenaline when she saw her special horse.

A very cautious groom was leading Banshee. The stallion, seeing the shoeing shed, reared back, eyes wide and staring.

Nikki gathered her crutch and stepped out of the golf cart, softly calling his name. Banshee pricked an ear in her direction. She hobbled up to the animal, took the rein from the groom. The stallion's velvet-soft nuzzle touched her cheek. She cooed his name, rubbing and patting his neck. "Gee, it's good to see you, big fellah," she said tearfully. "I sure missed you!"

Banshee snorted softly as if in reply.

"Now, are you going to be a good boy while we get that shoe on?"

"I sure do appreciate this, Miss Nikki," Clem said. "He's like a baby when you handle him."

She nodded. "Just as long as he doesn't think that I'm numbered among his persecutors!"

Banshee nuzzled Nikki's shoulder, puppylike, entreating her attention. She gave it to him fully while Clem took care of the job at hand.

Nikki didn't relish being present during shoeing. Clem favored hot shoeing over cold because he said the fit was always a little better. But as a shoe glowing red was carried from the coals to the anvil with tongs for customized hammering, Nikki quivered a little inside. It always seemed to her that the hot metal and driven nails were going to cause pain. But located as they were on the nonsensitive part of the hoof, she knew consciously that the horse felt nothing.

Clem did a slick, professional job as usual. When the task was completed, Nikki returned the reins to a groom, who took Banshee back to his stall.

With loving eyes, Nikki watched her prize three-year-old. The dreams of her lifetime had now come to a possible realization. It all depended on that beautiful animal. Then she glanced ruefully at the cast on her leg, reminding herself that the dream wasn't going to come true if she wasn't back in top riding form by the time of the big one—the Kentucky Derby this spring.

"Gee, that's something the way he acts around you, Mom," Johnny exclaimed with a touch of awe.

"Oh, we understand each other, just the way you and I do," she said, giving her son a hug. Then she started up the golf cart and continued on her inspection tour of the familiar grounds.

From the building area, Nikki turned her golf cart to the pastures. This was the part of the farm she loved the most. She could spend hours watching the thorough-breds and their colts grazing and cavorting with exuberant freedom in the open grasslands.

She followed a dirt path up a hill that had a special meaning to her. It was the highest elevation on Elmhurst Farms. From here she could see across acres of rolling pasture that stretched like a green carpet to the distant grazing lands of Crestland, the neighboring farm. From this distance, the great white mansion of Crestland was a tiny dollhouse nestled in the verdurous, undulating lands.

Nikki stopped the golf cart and clambered out, balancing her weight on the crutch as she gazed for long, wrenching moments at the land she had known as a child. She had been born in that house. Every inch of the pastureland was burned in her mind with bittersweet memory. She could never look at it without a tide of emotion, sadness and tearing anger. Crestland was her true home, not Elmhurst. No matter how much she loved Elvira and Elmhurst, the fact remained that she was a visitor here. How dare strangers take Crestland away from her, despoil her room with their presence, graze their horses on the lands that belonged to her ancestors! Crestland was as much a part of her as her hearbeat.

"See it, Johnny? That's our home."

"I know," the boy said, standing beside her, gazing at the distant buildings with serious dark eyes. Nikki had been bringing him to this spot since he was an infant.

"Someday we'll own it again, you and me," she said, repeating the old vow. She wanted it for her son, Johnny, every bit as much as for herself. Crestland should be his heritage. This was her great goal, her motive for carefully hoarding her earnings as a jockey. The purse from riding Spanish Lady across the winning line at Gulfstream would have put her a giant step closer to her goal. Now the only hope was riding Banshee to a win at the Kentucky Derby this spring.

"Tell me what it's like, Mom," Johnny asked, his eyes squinting at the distant land.

He'd heard the family stories a hundred times, but he never tired of her repeating them.

She wiped away the tears that were blurring her vision. The memory of her grandfather suddenly sprang alive, clear and sharp. Beauregard Stonewall Jackson. With his flowing mane of white hair and tall, courtly manner, he had been an incredible stereotype of the aristocratic southern "colonel." His father had fought with the Confederacy under Stonewall Jackson. Despite the same last names, he had not actually been related to the Civil War hero, but he had passed the name of his beloved general on to his son.

All those years came back. She remembered the stories her grandfather had told her about her forebears, about Crestland and all that the land had known, from the bloody travail of The War Between the States to the glory of raising Derby winners. Her ancestors for four generations were buried there in the private cemetery plot. Her grandfather slept there as did her mother, under the soil they loved.

She remembered how she had absorbed thoroughbred lore from the time she could toddle. She could hear
the echo of Orlis's voice from her childhood, telling her,
"Now, little Miss Nikki, raising thoroughbreds takes a
special kind of patience, love and dedication. They are
a very special kind of animal."

Nikki had learned all about the temperament of
thoroughbreds. Orlis had told her about the horses' su-
icidal tendencies. He had explained how they were
prone to shy from anything unknown and plunge
headlong into obstacles or conditions that meant certain injury. They could run themselves to death. A
bruised thoroughbred ego could have serious psycho-
somatic complications, bringing on a real illness. And
in keeping with such a high-strung temperament, they
were fussy eaters. They would go hungry rather than
touch grass they considered sour or unappetizing.

Nikki became an expert. She learned to size up a
pasture quickly. Grassland, she knew, had to be put to
rest part of each year. It had to have the right balance.
Thoroughbreds enjoyed rye grass, dandelion, cocks-
foot, fescue, timothy, ribgrass and bent grass. But there
were deadly varieties of vegetation that rooted tena-
ciously: yew, nightshade, hemlock, ragwort, laburnum
and foxglove. Poisonous plants must be pulled out by
the roots and burned. If left to wither and die in the
field, some of their deadly potency would remain. Pastures had to be kept free of objects that could damage
a hoof. Drainage had to be right lest a potential winner
slip and fall in mud. In winter, horses at pasture had to
be protected by a New Zealand rug, a special blanket.

And, she thought, the wrath of heaven on those careless motorists who tossed their emptied McDonald's sacks, Styrofoam cups and plastic bags from their cars! Wafted into a pasture on a breeze, a plastic bag was for some unknown reason attractive to a horse. If swallowed, the bag could be a passport of suffocation and death.

She put her arm around her son's shoulders and told him again the stories about her grandfather and about her very special childhood as she grew up at Crestland, surrounded by the adventure and thrill of thoroughbred racing until it became as much a part of her as the beat of her heart.

After a while, the memories of Crestland became too painful. Nikki turned away, got back in the golf cart and drove down to the main house.

She parked and hobbled into the building. "You run along and play for a while, Johnny. I want to see your granddad."

Down the hall from the office was a den, known in the era when the house was built as the "main parlor." Here were the trophy cases and framed photographs of Elmhurst champions.

In the spacious kitchen, a large staff had the daily task of preparing food for an active, ever-hungry staff that ranged from stable lads and equipment mechanics to a veterinarian at Elmhurst on a call that could keep him there for several days at a time. Often the kitchen took on the challenge of preparing special menus for a foreign client.

Only a horse farm aficionado could grasp the workings of the Elmhurst Farm. The nerve center was the large, secluded room in the east wing of the house designated as an office. It was a rather stark, no-frills sanctum furnished with gray steel desks and filing cabinets that showed the scuff of long wear. The oaken chairs and table showed the dull sheen of longtime human contact. A small computer stored the limitless bits of information unique to thoroughbreds and racing on which critical decisions were made. The TV screen of closed-circuit cameras offered round-the-clock access to the birthing barn during the foaling season.

This office was the headquarters of Nikki's father, Colby Cameron.

"Hi, Dad," Nikki greeted, coming into the room.

Colby glanced up from a sheath of papers on his desk. His eyes warmed. He quickly rose and came around the desk to give her hands a squeeze. "Nikki. It's good to see you up and around."

"It's good to be up and around." She nodded, settling into one of the easy chairs. "But good to sit down, too."

"Don't overdo it now," he said, frowning with concern. "You know the doctor said to take it easy at first."

"Oh, I am. Everybody is spoiling me. I guess you know about the golf cart Orlis had fixed up for me."

"Yeah." He grinned. "Orlis came to me with the idea, and I was all for it. Otherwise, knowing you, you'd try to hobble all over the place on a crutch."

The two exchanged a look of comfortable warmth and understanding.

It had not always been this way between Colby Cameron and his daughter. As a child, Nikki had barely known her father. Colby Cameron had married Annabelle Jackson, one of the most beautiful girls in Kentucky, shortly before the Korean War. Colby had volunteered for officer candidate school, graduated near the top of his class and had gone into action immediately and came out of the conflict a youthful lieutenant colonel, a field officer who was always first out of the aircraft when his paratroopers were assigned to a mission.

For a while, Cameron had followed a professional military career until Annabelle, fed up with army life, had given him an ultimatum. They moved back to Crestland, where Colby took over the job of training her father's string of thoroughbreds. Colby didn't have the aristocratic, plantation-owner background of the Jacksons. His background was of a much more humble social stratum. His father, a poor immigrant Irishman, had worked most of his life as a stable groom. From him, Colby had learned the skills of a thoroughbred trainer. Today, few trainers were more respected in the profession than Colby Cameron. His winners were a matter of record. His savvy of the thoroughbred spectrum was legend.

Nikki never knew what caused the final breakup between her father and mother. Apparently it had been a stormy marriage. Perhaps her mother's refusal to leave Crestland had something to do with it, or Colby's Irish temperament had clashed once too often with the proud, imperious, dictatorial nature of Beauregard Jackson, lord of the manor. It was a subject neither her mother nor her father would talk about. In any case, they were divorced before Nikki was three.

For a while, Colby simply disappeared. He went through a dark period involving a lot of empty bottles and dead-end streets, ending with a two-month stay in a roach-infested county jail for fistfighting and property damage in a beer joint. Something to do with his hitting a jukebox with a chair because it wouldn't play "Honky Tonk Angel" after swallowing his quarter. The incarceration had a sobering effect on Colby. He stopped trying to drink all the sour mash in Kentucky, straightened up and got a job in the profession he knew best, horse training. Eventually, an ironic fate brough him almost full circle to Elmhurst, next door to Crestland.

It was about that time when tragic events turned Nikki's life upside down. A series of unwise investments, an epidemic of illnesses among his horses, not to mention a crooked trainer who cost him some races, brought her grandfather to the brink of bankruptcy. Then a stroke robbed him of the ability to cope with the situation, and Crestland went on the auction block. Beauregard Stonewall Jackson only lived long enough to be buried in the family plot before his land changed hands. Before the year ended, Nikki's mother fell victim to a sudden illness and was laid to rest in the same plot. It was as if the proud Jacksons couldn't live without Crestland and so had forever become part of the land they loved so fervently.

Nikki then had only one place to go live—with her father, her only living relative. Colby suddenly found himself the sole parent of a resentful, angry teenager. Nikki had inherited the Irish temper of the Camerons and the aristocratic stubbornness of the Jacksons, a volatile combination exacerbated by what she considered a rotten deal by life.

During his drinking days, Colby had deliberately stayed out of Nikki's life. After he got his own life straightened out, he saw her a few times but by then they were strangers, awkward and reserved with each other.

When she came to live with him, Colby was at a loss to know how to go about being a father. In those days, Nikki had been as wild as an unbroken colt. Horses and racing were her obsession. At Crestland, her grandfather had encouraged her riding talent. She had gotten considerable publicity as a child trick rider at horse shows. Her riding skill had taken her over obstacles at steeplechase matches. But it was the thrill of racing that most fascinated her. And for a while it was a form of escape from the bitterness and grief of losing her grandfather, mother and home all in a year's time.

She ran away from Elmhurst more than once. Colby would find her in a quarter-horse race in some outlaw track in Texas or in a rodeo in New Mexico and drag her kicking and howling back to Elmhurst.

He spent a good deal of his time and money bailing her out of trouble. When she wasn't racing horses she was chasing around the countryside with a high-school boyfriend, Brad Hall, breaking speeding laws and flunking high-school courses. It was inevitable that they would rack up Brad's MG, which in due course they did, managing in the process to involve several patrol cars in a two-county high-speed chase. How they walked away from the steaming, twisted wreckage of Brad's red sports car was a miracle Colby could only ascribe to a kind guardian angel while he scratched desperately for the money and influential friends to keep Nikki from serving time in a juvenile correction institution.

Only his compassion for the rough hand life had dealt her at such a vulnerable age gave him the forbearance to get her out of the mess.

"You're impossible, you know that?" Colby had exploded when he'd bailed her out of the juvenile detention hall. "I ought to take you across my knee and give your bottom a good dusting!"

"Yeah?" she'd said, her eyes blazing back defiance. "Just try!"

When it was that she'd come to love the gruff, earthy man who was her father, Nikki wasn't sure. She had a grudging admiration and respect for his knowledge of horseflesh and the things she could learn from him in her quest to become a jockey. Somewhere along the way the admiration and respect had turned into love.

Now Colby asked, "Have you seen Banshee?"

"First thing early this morning. He had to be shoed. Clem was glad to see me."

"I'll bet he was! That stallion turns into a raging fury when the farrier comes around. Did he give you any trouble?"

"None at all. He's just like a big baby with me cuddling him." She hesitated, frowning down at her cast. Suddenly she slapped it with a frustrated gesture. "Damn! I wanted to ride him in the prep races."

"Don't worry about it. He'll do okay."

"But not as well as he would carrying me."

"Well, you'll be okay in time for the Derby. That's what counts."

"Yeah," she said absently, fingering the cast. Her body would be healed by then. But would there be other, deeper wounds, still raw and festering? Every time she thought about that dreadful moment at Gulf-stream when she was flung through the air, her palms got sweaty and tension tightened her stomach, clouding her thinking. There was no room for that kind of distraction while competing in the Derby.

This wasn't the first time she had been injured. In one of the early races after she got her license, when she was still an apprentice, a skittish mount had reared back and fallen on her, breaking several ribs. A collarbone had also been broken when she was thrown from a bronco in a western rodeo. The bones had barely knitted before she was back in a saddle. This time it was different in a way she couldn't quite analyze. Something had gone deeper than the broken bones and bruised flesh.

A shudder run through her. With an effort, she pushed the black thoughts away.

Colby had moved to his desk. He sat on the edge, absently fingering a gold-plated horseshoe paper-weight. He picked it up, looked at it and put it down. He cleared his throat, glanced at Nikki, then picked up the paperweight again.

An amused smile tugged at Nikki's lips. "What in the world is bothering you?"

"What?" Colby asked blankly.

"Come on, Dad. There's something on your mind. What is it?"

He cleared his throat again. "What makes you think there's something on my mind?"

"Well, it's pretty obvious."

He nodded, looking uncomfortable. "Yeah, as a matter of fact, there is something I wanted to tell you." He moved away from the desk, stared out the window for a moment as if mentally arranging his words, then turned to face her again. "Nikki, this is a delicate subject. I don't want to upset you. But...well, Jacques Trenchard is back in the States."

Nikki felt a rush of blood to her cheeks. Her gaze faltered. "I—I know, Dad," she stammered. "I saw him in the crowd at Gulfstream just before the race. When I was in the hospital, he sent me some flowers."

Colby chewed his lip, looking disturbed. "Did he tell you why he's here?"

"I...didn't talk to him. He just sent the flowers with his card. There was no message. I—I thought he'd flown back to Europe by now...."

Colby uttered a short laugh. "Hardly. He's going to be our next-door neighbor, Nikki. Jacques Trenchard has just bought Crestland."

Chapter Four

For a moment after her father dropped the bombshell, Nikki was too stunned to react. It was as if all her senses were frozen. Slowly, her shocked mind accepted the words. Jacques...the owner of Crestland.

"I—I don't understand," she gasped.

Colby shrugged. "I guess he made the present co-op owners an offer they couldn't refuse. From the gossip I've heard, he paid through the nose for the place."

She felt groggy, like a fighter who had taken a hard punch. Questions exploded in her mind. What would possess Jacques to buy Crestland? What was his motivation? What did this mean to her life? And then a fresh thought sent a chill through her—her son, Johnny. How was this surprising development going to affect him?

Her thoughts spun backward to that dreadful day almost six years ago when Jacques Trenchard had walked into her life. It was July. She was twenty and had already applied for her jockey license. She had accompanied her father to Keeneland, one of the most prestigious of thoroughbred auctions.

A corner of her heart was always saddened that at the annual event horses were traded in exchange for money. They were bought and sold. It didn't seem quite right for a thoroughbred. But it was a fact of life and there was the consoling thought that anyone who bought a Keeneland yearling would cherish and protect the investment.

In the days preceding the sale, humming Elmhurst had devoted special attention to the half-dozen yearlings to be offered, each of which must have a glittering pedigree and pass a rigorous conformation inspection just to be eligible for the auctioneer's block. Carefully trained, immaculately groomed, the four hundred or so yearlings to be sold would reach Fasig-Tipton's Newtown Paddocks the day before the sale. Each yearling would have its private stall in the vast fly-free, pristine yearling barn where pedigree cards and hip number notations identified entries in the catalog.

Strangers from every corner of the Western world, some bringing along English-speaking translators, would inspect the horses, marking numbers occasionally in the catalog. Most counted their money in millions, if they bothered to count it at all. But here and there the small breeder, dreaming of a champion among the passed-over yearlings, would rub shoulders with an Argentine land owner, an oil-rich Arab sheikh, a British member of the House of Lords, or an Italian movie mogul.

While employees communicated via walkie-talkies, yearlings with trainers and chief grooms would go into the walking ring four or five at a time in rotation by hip number. When the hip number was called for sale, an employee would lead the yearling down the chute into the amphitheater. Then the no-holds-barred money war for horseflesh would begin, the auctioneer earning his five percent of the sale by chanting from the high, white podium.

Colby told Nikki that the present, almost savage selling techniques had been perfected back in the 1940s by the team of George Swineboard, auctioneer, and Humphrey Finney, announcer, who goaded, joked, flattered, played ego against ego to encourage competitive bidding.

Nikki couldn't believe there could be so much money in the world. Each year the prices went higher. Who a generation ago could possibly dream that Fabuleuse Jane, an offspring of Northern Dancer, would go in the 1984 yearling sale to Sheikh Mohammed al-Maktoum for more than seven million dollars? That was an exorbitant amount of money to risk on an untried yearling subject to everything from colic to bronchitis, flu, tetanus or pneumonia, not to mention pulled tendons, tender knees or cracked hooves.

That fateful day, amidst the hustle and bustle of the auction grounds, Nikki had left the paddock where Elmhurst yearlings were safely enstalled under the watchful eyes of capable grooms. She started along the concourse, going to join her father in the offices and get a cup of coffee. As she walked, she soaked up the ambience surrounding her, the mingled smells of sweet hay, manure, humid horseflesh. She loved the feeling of excitement in the air. She especially loved being surrounded by so many beautiful thoroughbreds.

As she passed stall number six, a soft whicker reached out to her. She stopped, turned and looked into the big brown eyes of a sleek black filly. The yearling flicked its ears and lifted flaring nostrils in her direction.

"Hi, there, you beautiful girl!" Nikki's heart melted. She was drawn involuntarily toward the entreating eyes. "Don't be lonely," she said comfortingly. "Everyone is a little frightened at first in a strange place, even a princess like you."

Clad in wrinkled coveralls, hair tucked up under her old baseball cap, Nikki cut a slightly baggy, nondescript figure as she reached an arm through one of the slatted openings in the stall to give the homesick filly a touch on the muzzle.

"Sure, of course you understand," she went on soothingly. "Everyone here loves you, and—"

Suddenly an angry male voice interrupted her, causing a twitching and shuffling among the hay-floored stalls. "Hey, you! You—the boy at stall number six!"

Nikki jerked her arm back and spun around to face the angry man striding toward her.

"What do you think you're doing?" he demanded. "How did you get past security to one of my stalls?"

He was a whipcord-lean six-footer, one of those wire-and-leather men built to grind an adversary to nothing on a tennis court or outride an opponent on a polo field. The bone structure of his face was chiseled in aristocratic lines. Above a high, wide forehead was a sweep of coal-black hair. His complexion was olive. Large black eyes were ablaze, lean nostrils flared.

His hand clamped on her shoulder. He gave her a shake that caused her teeth to snap.

Her reaction to such manhandling would normally have been a kicking, biting counterattack. But she looked up at the handsome face of Jacques Trenchard and her heart turned over and tumbled into a wild nothingness where only those striking masculine features were real.

His grip hurt, though she stubbornly refused to flinch. Lightning flashed through her mind as well as heart. For a fleeting moment she wondered what it would be like to have that hand touching her in a caress.

She writhed out of his grip and bounced a step backward. "Calm down! I'm from Elmhurst Farms, with every bit as much right here as you. I was just giving that lonely little girl a friendly pat."

Looking at his face with a bit more clarity, she gauged his age at some ten years older than herself. She saw the vigor of the outdoors in a face that was tanned and slightly weathered. The jet black of his hair indicated the kind of dark beard that had to be shaved twice a day if he were going out for a special evening.

The sound of her voice had stopped him cold. Looking momentarily confused, he touched the scruffy baseball cap. It slipped from her head and her hair tumbled down around her face, bringing a gasp from him.

He took a step backward, his gaze ranging from her head to her sneakered toes. He uttered a soft exclamation to himself in French.

Nikki's cheeks colored. "Listen, if you've got something to say to me, speak in English. If I'm to be insulted for my appearance, I want to understand it."

He threw back his head and laughed uproariously, showing a flash of even white teeth. "Pardon me, mam'selle. I was just saying to myself what a treasure of young womanhood beneath those grubby clothes. From the back, I mistook you for a boy."

Nikki met his gaze with cool, leveled eyes. She drew a breath, causing her bosom to strain against the fabric of her outer garment. She raised her chin. "And from the front?"

The man looked at her, his lips turned in an amused smile. "From the front there is certainly no way anyone could make that kind of mistake. Again, forgive me. My name is Jacques Trenchard."

She found his slight accent fascinating. "French, right?"

He bowed his head slightly in an affirmative gesture. "And your name?"

She experienced a momentary wave of unexplainable shyness. "Nikki...Cameron...."

Trenchard pursed his lips thoughtfully. "Cameron...Cameron. That name sounds very familiar. Are you related to Colby Cameron?"

"He's my father."

"Ah." Again that flashing smile that gave her a weak sensation in her knees. "That explains the color of your hair and the temper in your eyes. I guess I got off lucky.

If you're like your father, I could have gotten a kick where it really hurts.''

"I was thinking about it," she said disdainfully. "I'm very much like my father—except in certain ways."

His amused gaze trailed boldly down the healthy young curves of her body, making her face tingle. "Yes, I can see the difference."

His boldness put her instinctively on guard while at the same time awakening again the tingle that raced over her flesh. Now that she knew his name, she could identify him. Jacques Trenchard was well known in thoroughbred circles as well as in the international social and financial world. He was a wealthy young jet-setter, one of Europe's most eligible and exciting bachelors. She had seen his name often in gossip tabloids. It was impossible not to be flattered at the obvious interest in the eyes of such a man. She felt a feminine self-awareness that belied her tomboy appearance.

"I've always heard Frenchmen were fast," she said, a certain warning challenge in her eyes.

"Fast? You mean on a horse or in a car race?"

"You know what I mean. With women."

"We very quickly appreciate beautiful women, if that's what you mean." He chuckled.

She stood there a moment longer, relishing the tingly glow his attention gave her. Then she said, "Well, nice to have met you. I was on my way to have a cup of coffee with my father."

"Is he expecting you?"

"Not exactly. Why?"

"I thought perhaps you could have a drink with me, Nikki.''

His casual use of her first name caught her strangely off guard. She regained some emotional equilibrium and tried to sound casual as she replied, "Okay."

"Good." His warm look of pleasure at her acceptance set her aglow.

They were an unlikely looking couple seated in the clubhouse at Keeneland—Jacques in the smart, casual attire of a continental gentleman, Nikki in her rumpled coveralls, baseball cap thrust into a back pocket.

She glanced around the sumptuous clubroom that was humming busily while at the same time retaining its subdued air. The patrons today were mostly buyers, owner-breeder sellers. A nonmillionaire would be the exception rather than the rule. Patrons nibbled and sipped and huddled in low-toned talk that revolved around pedigrees, conformations, possible prices, outside bids. Among them were purchasing agents for absentee thoroughbred lovers, Hollywood moguls, European industrialists, owners of international shipping companies. Those empowered to purchase for the absentee would sleep little tonight, poring over figures and tying up long-distance and overseas telephone numbers for last minute computations, decisions and bid ceilings.

Jacques asked, "Would you care for a glass of wine, or are you old enough? Perhaps a soft drink—"

Color rose to her cheek. "Old enough?" she repeated with an angry, challenging tilt of her chin. "Of course. A glass of wine would be perfect."

"Very well." He ordered two glasses of Chablis blanc.

As he spoke to the waitress, Nikki stole a closer look at his face. He had nice eyebrows, dark and masculine, with a faint crease in between the brows and above the bridge of his nose. A clean-lined jaw indicated that he could be stubborn. No wonder women fell all over themselves at his glance. Careful, girl, she thought.

She realized he had spoken to her. "Sorry. You were saying?"

"I was asking where we are having dinner."

"I didn't know we were."

Boy, she thought, he's a smooth one. Not at all like the high-school boys she'd dated or some of the crude men who hung around the tracks. This man had been around. He was totally relaxed, radiating confidence in his own masculinity—a very dangerous quality in a man.

"You must have dinner with me," he insisted. "You're not going to deny me the chance to show you I'm not altogether the ogre who yelled at you in the yearling barn."

"Oh, you don't have to apologize for that. You had every right to challenge a stranger around your horses. I'd have done the same thing myself."

A waitress came with two small glasses of white wine. He raised his glass. "To an unexpected meeting that has turned into a delightful experience."

His gaze moved from her face along her slender neck to the small pulse in her throat. It was as if he were unsnapping the coverall slowly, one snap at a time, laying back the poplin cloth, letting the light have full play on the firm but softly contoured rise of her breasts.

A maidenly part of her wanted to blush in embarrassment, to seethe in indignation at his boldness. But at the same time there awakened in her a sensation dizzying and breath-catching, a kind of primeval arousal. She was aware of the restraint of the poplin against the rise of her breasts, the faint hardening of her nipples.

Then she managed to step aside mentally and catch a look at herself. Color deepening in her eyes, lips moist and parted. Silly fool! Jacques Trenchard was obviously a lady-killer. He was just amusing himself by turning his continental charm on a vulnerable youngster.

His eyes swept the room, observing everything from a white turban inset with an emerald above a swarthy face to Gucci shirts and blouses to hand-tailored cashmere sports jackets, then returned to her coveralls. He couldn't restrain a laugh. There was nothing phony or synthetic about his laugh, Nikki thought. When he laughed, he meant it. When he threw back his head, it was a hearty laugh, no matter how quietly unobtrusive he managed to keep the sound.

"*Mon Dieu*! How adorable you are, Nikki!" He shook his head. "I surrender. I give up. You are beyond analyzing."

He reached, took her hand and leaned over the table a little closer to her. "You know, with that little smudge on your cheek, you've no right at all to wear those—what is the American slang?—cotton-pickin' coveralls. They were never meant to be so darn sexy."

The touch of his fingers against hers was a contact point for the release of pulsing, low-voltage electricity. She had never felt this way before, never experienced this smothery sensation in her throat. Was he feeling the same thing? Was that the cause of the smoky shadows swirling in his eyes?

This was plain insanity. They were strangers. She knew what people thought of her, that Nikki Cameron was a wild teenager. The reputation was well deserved. So maybe she liked to chase around with Brad Hall, drive fast, stay up all night, do crazy things like go skinny-dipping on a cold winter night. But there were limits; she was plain scared of the crazy feelings Jacques Trenchard was arousing in her.

She had seen it happen to some of her friends, girls suddenly drugged with "instant love"—infatuation was a better description—girls unable to think of anything but a certain boy they'd just met, girls who plunged in, succumbed without thinking. But they should have heeded the lyrics in an old Cole Porter song about affairs that were too hot not to cool down. In almost every case, the girls had ended up shattered and picking up the pieces alone.

She wasn't going to fall into that old trap—not with this continental charmer, as delicious as his gaze and touch could make her feel. There was too much at stake. She had worked too hard, made too many sacrifices to earn her jockey license to get sidetracked. Her big moment was at hand, the horses she was going to ride, the races she was going to win.

With an effort, she gained some control of her rampant emotions and stood up. "Well, thanks for the drink. I have to get back to our horses."

"You're not going to forget about our dinner engagement?"

"I—I don't know. I've got a lot to do, helping dad at our stalls...."

His smile was cool and assured. "We can't let a little thing like that get in the way, can we? I'll drop by later this evening."

It was a statement, not a question. Nikki wiped her suddenly damp palms down the sides of her coveralls. She didn't know exactly what kind of reply to make, so she just turned and fled.

That guy shakes me up, she thought, walking blindly in the direction of the Elmhurst horse stalls. She'd never before been so disturbed by a member of the male sex. Was it because he was an older man showing an obvious interest in her? Not only older, but sophisticated, cosmopolitan, continental. That could turn any girl's head! She wouldn't be much of a female if she didn't feel flattered by the interest shown by such a man. Maybe that was what put the butterflies in her stomach. She didn't have the experience to cope with this kind of attraction. She had the scary feeling that a force had been unleashed that could take control of her life. She didn't want that. Her life was carefully planned. Ahead of her was a challenge that would test her heart and soul to the limit, the bitter struggle for recognition in a man's world, the racetrack. There was no room in the scenario for a romantic entanglement getting in the way.

That afternoon she stayed busy, trying unsuccessfully to keep thoughts of Jacques Trenchard from churning through her mind. Was he going to come around bothering her for that dinner date again? She had as good as turned him down.

She was on tenterhooks, half hoping, half dreading his putting in another appearance. And when he didn't, the emotion changed to relief tinged with more than just a shade of disappointment. A part of her chided; You should have your head examined, girl. How could a woman in her right mind turn down a dinner date with a charming hunk like that? Well, she thought, she hadn't exactly turned him down. She'd been confused and unsure of herself and had given him a vague reply. If he were really interested, he would have come back to make sure about the date. Better forget the whole incident.

Easier said than done!

Shortly before sunset, she became aware of a small commotion at one end of the barn. She stepped out from behind a stall and blinked, not believing what she was seeing.

Coming in her direction was a small entourage consisting of a pair of waiters with white linen napkins draped over their forearms, two busboys in mess jackets, each pushing a service cart, a third holding a folding chair under each arm and two more carrying a small, narrow table between them.

Looking blindingly handsome in a beautifully tailored dinner jacket was Jacques Trenchard, leading the group.

Grooms came out of stalls to stare open-mouthed.

The parade came to a halt in front of Nikki. They all appeared to be enjoying themselves immensely, springing into quick, professional action to whisk a white linen cloth on the table, unfold the chairs, then arrange place settings for two with fine china, crystal and silver. From the cart a busboy produced a centerpiece of fresh flowers. Then they took their stations.

Jacques' eyes were sparkling mischievously. He greeted Nikki with a short bow, then demoralized her completely with a continental kiss on her hand. "Since you said you might be too busy to leave your barn for dinner, I thought I'd bring dinner to you."

The bizarre event, reflecting Jacques's offbeat sense of humor, should have warned her. The dinner ushered in a fantasy too overpowering for her to cope with.

In retrospect, she tried to understand the girl who, until Jacques Trenchard walked into her life, thought she had her destiny pretty well in hand.

Years later, during quiet moments, Nikki would try to clarify in her mind the girl who'd dined that evening with Jacques Trenchard. Upon reflection she would see more clearly the two people in the yearling barn. She, the country kid, foolish in her inexperience and Jacques, the older man of the world, playing a game at which he was skilled.

Her background was a curious mixture. Part of it was horse stables and racetracks ranging from outlaw quarter-horse tracks in the backwoods of Oklahoma to Belmont Park. Part of it was Elmhurst, where the comings and goings were frequently international, as well as the Kentucky country clubs and the wealthy horsey set. Her worldly knowledge included such earthy experiences as helping with the birth of a colt. She knew which fork to use at a formal dinner table, but she also knew how to hold a yearling's infected foot in a bucket of hot Epsom salts water.

But with all of that, when it came to playing the adult game of love between a man and a woman, she was pretty naive.

How romantic that dinner had seemed! She felt surrounded by a golden haze, as if special lighting had created a dreamy ambience for a movie scene. There was an iced bucket of champagne. The meal, catered by one of Louisville's finest restaurants, included crisp salad tossed before her eyes, Lobster newburg, delicious vegetables and, finally, French pastries and coffee.

She felt Jacques's gaze throughout the meal. Her fingers holding her fork trembled. She was acutely conscious of his presence. Out of the corner of her eye, she saw his strong, tanned fingers handle his knife and fork. When he raised a glass of champagne to toast her, then brought the bubbling liquid to his smiling lips, her heart thudded. Never, never had she been so aware of a man. Everything about him impinged on her senses, the aroma of his shaving lotion, the rustle of his dinner jacket as he moved, the masculine timbre of his voice. A kind of kinetic charge surrounded him, making the air fairly crackle. She felt drawn to him, wanting to touch him.

He spoke, bringing her spinning thoughts together. "Let's become better acquainted, Nikki," he said. "Tell me about yourself. You appear to love horses very much."

"That's all I've known all my life. Horses *are* my life."

Jacques smiled. "We have much in common. I, too, love horses. And, of course, the excitement of the polo field and the racetrack."

"Yes, the racetrack." Nikki's eyes brightened. "I'm a jockey."

"A jockey?" For a moment he looked as if he didn't believe her. He regarded her with an expression of amused incredulity. "You're joking, of course. Pulling my leg, as you Americans say?"

She frowned. "No, I'm not joking."

"But you can't be serious!"

Her face became flushed as she bridled. "And why not?"

"But a jockey! Pardon me, but that's a man's profession."

Now he was getting her Irish up. "Well, you male chauvinist!" she spluttered. "Where have you been the last ten years? Don't you know there are some very competent, successful women jockeys? Mary Bacon, Robyn Smith, Patty Barton..."

"Yes, of course I know. But it's such a dangerous profession. Nearly three hundred jockeys get injured every year. Some are killed, some crippled for life."

"So do airplane pilots and lots of them are women."

"Aside from the danger," he went on, "top jockeys have to be superb athletes. They have to have the strength to control a horse weighing half a ton plunging down a crowded track. How can a slip of a girl like yourself—"

Nikki's eyes were flashing angrily. "I've been on horses since I could walk. Before I was fourteen, I raced Appaloosas in the outlaw bush tracks in Texas and Oklahoma, where jockeys think nothing of carrying chains or using illegal electric buzzers to make their mounts go faster. I could outride you any day of the week!''

He chuckled tolerantly, which only infuriated her more. She struggled to keep her voice under control. ''And there's more than just brute strength involved. Women have a way with horses, a communication and rapport with thoroughbreds better than most men.''

''Well, perhaps.'' He shrugged. ''That's debatable.''

''I doubt it,'' she said coldly. He'd touched a sore spot with her and fury churned through her. ''It makes my blood boil when I think about the discrimination women have had to deal with on the racetrack. Do you know until a few years ago it was impossible for a woman to get a jockey license? They've been hiring women for years to do the dirty work and the menial jobs around the horse barns. Women are natural grooms, exercise riders, hot walkers and stable foremen. Not many men will do that kind of work for the low wages they pay. Trainers had to hire winos and drifters who wouldn't show up half the time. Then they put women on the payroll and found out that they were more dependable and got along better with the horses.''

''Nikki—''

But he'd gotten her furious and couldn't stop her emotional outburst. ''But just let a woman get out of the stable and apply for a jockey license and she runs smack up against track secretaries, stewards, commissioners, jockey associations, owners and trainers and their associations, all of them male and all stubbornly determined not to allow a woman to trespass on their territory. It wasn't until the Olympic rider Kathy Kusner took it to court and won the right to ride in the state of Maryland that the barriers began to fall. After Kathy there was Penny Ann Early. Four times she tried to ride at Churchill Downs. She was boycotted by male jockeys and accused by the press of publicity seeking. Then in 1969, Diane Crump showed them all. In Charles Town, West Virginia, she rode the colt Cohesian to victory before a record-breaking crowd, the first woman in sports history to beat men in a professional sport.''

Nikki paused for breath, but before Jacques could say anything, she continued, ''They finally had to allow women on the tracks, but we still have to battle against sex discrimination. More than in any other field. There was prejudice everywhere, everything from denial of use of jockey's facilities so a female jockey had to change into her silks in the women's restrooms to being fouled in a race by male jockeys who were sure the stewards would either look the other way or take their side against a woman if charges were brought.

''The only way a lot of us could get started was to get a van, a sleeping bag and a Coleman stove and do the circuit of outlaw tracks, the country fairs, the rodeos, fighting for enough gas money to get to the next stand.

''Things are a little better now. There've been enough competent women jockeys to pave the way. They can't refuse to license us any longer, though we still often have to change in the women's dressing room, listen to abuse from male jockeys and put up with sexual harassment from some trainers and owners.''

A chill had fallen over the evening. Jacques tried to salvage the romantic mood by changing the subject, but it was too late. Nikki was too angry.

Realizing the matter wasn't going to heal itself, he said, "Nikki, forgive me if I've hurt your feelings."

"You haven't hurt my feelings. You've made me furious."

"Well, I didn't mean to. You caught me by surprise."

"Because I said I was a jockey?"

"Yes. It's the last thing I expected."

"I suppose girl jockeys are still something of an oddity," she admitted. "But it's your superior male attitude that makes me angry. If you think I can't ride, come out to the tracks tomorrow night. I'll be riding in the fifth." She saw no reason to tell him that it was going to be her first professional race as an apprentice jockey.

He pursed his lips thoughtfully. "Of course I'll be there, Nikki. I certainly intend seeing you again."

His dark eyes caught her gaze with a power that suddenly made her quiver.

Chapter Five

A girl jockey?"

André Broussard chuckled as he helped himself to a piece of toast from Jacques' breakfast tray.

"Yes, a girl jockey." Jacques smiled at his lifelong friend.

"Well, why not? Let me see, there was that English movie scriptwriter. And of course Margaret, the Swiss ski instructor." André scowled. "As I recall, you took that one away from me. Anyway, why not an American girl jockey? Should be amusing."

It was the morning after Jacques had brought the dinner to Nikki's barn at the auction. André had dropped by Jacques' hotel suite. Jacques was still in a dressing gown, having breakfast. The two friends were talking comfortably in French.

Jacques said, "I don't think you understand, my friend. This one is different."

"Yes, I know. They all are at first." André scooped a liberal helping of jelly onto the toast.

"Are you sure you don't want me to have a tray sent up for you?"

"No, no. A little of that coffee and I'll be fine."

"You've already eaten all the toast and the grapefruit."

"Keeping you from getting fat, my friend."

"Thank you very much," Jacques said dryly.

He watched with amusement as André devoured the last of the toast, washing it down with the remainder of the coffee. He and André had been friends since prep school. Their families had close ties going back several generations. Jacques often thought of André as a brother. Their interests were alike; they were both athletic. They had raced yachts, skied in the Alps, driven at Le Mans. Tennis and polo were their favorite games. In appearance they differed. André was built along heavier lines and his light brown hair and blue eyes were a contrast to Jacques' jet-black hair and olive complexion.

André, too, was a lover of thoroughbreds. Like Jacques' family, the Broussards owned a stable of fine horses. He also had come to Keeneland to do some horse-trading.

His appetite satisfied, André snapped a platinum lighter and touched the flame of his cigarette, then settled comfortably into the pillows on the couch. "So tell me about your latest affair of the heart, Jacques."

Jacques' eyes blazed. "I don't know how I can describe her, André. She's like no one I've met before. Lovely to look at, of course."

"Of course. Jacques Trenchard's mam'selles are all lovely."

"Not beautiful, exactly. That healthy American look. You've seen it. Suntanned. A hint of freckles."

"A bit of a tomboy, yes? I'm not surprised. A lady horseback racer...."

Restlessly, Jacques arose and paced to and fro, rubbing the back of his neck. "It's more than the looks, André. An inner fire—a strength and independence like an unbroken colt. An earthy quality, too, yet a sensitivity. When I met her, she was comforting one of my yearlings that she thought was frightened. She was wearing coveralls and a baseball cap. I yelled at her, thinking she was a boy trespassing in my barn. Then she turned around and...and...she's adorable, André. Simply adorable."

With a contemplative expression, André watched his friend's restless movements. "I've never seen you quite this worked up over a female, Jacques," he said slowly.

"I've never met anyone like Nikki Cameron before."

"Good heavens, you're not thinking of getting serious, are you?"

"It's entirely possible. Give me one of your cigarettes."

André handed him a gold case. "You just met the girl yesterday and you say it could be serious? Jacques, are you sure one of your yearlings didn't kick you in the head?"

"I tell you this, André. When you meet a girl like Nikki, you feel like you've been kicked by a horse or run over by a train."

André shook his head. "Jacques. Dammit, man, you're beginning to scare me. You're over here to buy horses for the Trenchard stables, not go home with a lady jockey. You want your grandmother to have a stroke?"

Jacques smiled wryly. "I don't think I would cause any twinges in Grandmother's aristocratic sensitivities. Nikki's pedigree is as thoroughbred as the horses she rides. On her mother's side she comes from a very old, aristocratic Kentucky family, the Jacksons. Not that I would give a hang if her parents were carnival freaks."

"Good Lord, you do have it bad. You met the girl yesterday and you are actually making sounds like an idiot who is contemplating marriage."

Jacques shrugged. "Who knows? Could be. It's true we need to become better acquainted, but I tell you, André, there is something to an instant, overwhelming attraction. I could barely keep my hands off her. I hardly slept a wink last night and, when I did, I dreamed about her."

"You're a damn fool, Jacques, you know that? Have an affair with the girl. That's the best cure for that instant attraction you're talking about. Sleep with her a few times, get your head back on straight, buy your string of yearlings and go home. In a few weeks, we'll have a big laugh about this over a glass of champagne at the Café Beautreux."

Jacques shook his head, his face serious. "She's not the type to settle for that, André, and I'm not sure I would want it that way, either. After we see each other some more and become better acquainted and if I still feel this way, I would want to take her back with me as my wife. She's only twenty, by the way."

André threw up his hands. "Now I've heard everything. Not only have you got yourself a lady jockey, but you're robbing the cradle."

"She's a very mature twenty. A girl growing up around the racetrack crowd becomes an adult at an early age."

"I suppose there would be an advantage to having a wife who is a jockey. She would be able to give you some hot inside tips on where to lay your bets."

"Don't be sarcastic. Anyway, if things work out between us, I'm going to have to talk her out of this jockey thing. It's entirely too dangerous for a girl. I'm sure once I take her to Europe, introduce her to our crowd, show her the Riviera, take her skiing in the Alps, go sightseeing in Rome, gamble at Monte Carlo, she'll forget all about this silly notion of risking her pretty neck against tough male jockeys on thoroughbreds running pell-mell down a dirt racetrack."

Nikki was at that very moment on a dirt track giving an early morning workout to a thoroughbred named Altogether.

A beginning jockey learns his trade under the tutelage of a licensed owner or trainer. As an apprentice, the jockey remains under contract to the trainer for several years. According to the racing rules in most states, the apprentice is not employed by his boss, the trainer. Rather, he has "bound himself" to his boss and can be ordered to work seven days a week at a variety of menial stable jobs when he isn't racing. When he does race, the trainer decides which mounts the jockey will ride.

Nikki was fortunate to have as her teacher her father, Colby Cameron, one of the most respected and successful trainers in the state. But Colby didn't go easy on her just because she was his daughter. He made her work as hard as any apprentice who had signed on with him.

Behind the glamour of the silks and the moment of glory—coming down the homestretch, fighting for the lead—were long hours of hard, dirty work like getting up at dawn to clean stalls, soap leather bridles, saddles and halters and gallop the trainer's horses around the practice ring.

Nikki was hardly aware of her chores during the day. She could think of nothing except the race she would ride that night. It would be her first real race as an apprentice jockey.

When a jockey applied for a license, his first two races are watched closely by the track stewards. How he performs in those first races could determine whether or not he'll get the license. That made this race all important to Nikki.

She had to ride a good race to prove to the stewards that she was competent enough to be granted a license. She had to prove it to herself. She had to prove that she was equal to the male competition.

Nikki knew that the women pioneers who had preceded her had paved the way for her to ride tonight. She could imagine what the conversation would have sounded like if she had applied for a license back in the days before Kathy Kusner took the matter to court:

You want to be a jockey, lady? You've got to be kidding. That's a man's job.

Why?

You're a girl.

What kind of reason is that?

Reason enough. What are you, some kind of freak? Who ever heard of a woman in a horse race?

But women generally have a little better rapport with horses than men.

Maybe, when it comes to grooming, exercising, that kind of thing.

Then why not racing?

Lady, you're talking about the physical strength to control a thousand pounds of sometimes nearly berserk animal in a pack of other berserkers.

I'm as strong as any hundred-and-five-pound man.

Oh, yeah? Look, you want a job around the barn, I can use you there. I'll pay you minimum wage to muck out the stables.

Yeah, I know all about that. You're glad to get us because we'll work cheaper than men and because we happen to love thoroughbreds and the way of life. Now it's time to give us a shot at the racing silks.

Now look, sweetheart. I've told you. Your apprentice application has been turned down. Go do it like sensible women, in horse shows and on sulky tracks.

Maybe I'm not very sensible, but I don't care for what you're offering.

The pioneer female jockeys met the prejudice head-on, giving her this chance. She was proud of them. That was Nikki Cameron's heritage for better or worse. And tonight she would be breaking down her own barriers to the career she wanted.

Before the race that night, Colby talked with her briefly about the strategy of horse racing. "Nikki, most thoroughbreds usually can run only a quarter of a mile or so at top speed. A good jockey has to pick the best time to unleash the burst of speed. A lot depends on the length of the race, what your horse can do and what your opposition is. You can't wait too long, but you don't want to turn your mount loose when there's a bunched field directly ahead of you. And you'll waste it going wide around a turn. If you're leading the pack on a fast nag, he might have plenty in reserve to beat any challengers when you near the finish line. On the other hand, you'll find that some horses have a tendency to pull themselves up when they get out in front. If you're riding one like that, you've got to time it so you make your move out front just as you reach the finish line. That takes experience and real riding skill.

"Now this is the maiden race for the horse I'm putting you on tonight. There are heavy odds against her, but I think she's got a good chance against the favorite and I'll tell you why. The track is sloppy. Tonight's favorite usually runs a come-from-behind race, and he does better on a fast track. He doesn't like slop thrown back in his face. The track you're on tonight is better for a speed horse who can take the lead early and has the stamina to hold it. That's the way I want you to handle this race. Try to take the lead as soon as you're out of the gate and hold it. I know this horse. He won't let you down."

Colby scooped up his daughter in powerful arms and tossed her up on her mount, a big black brute of a stallion named, appropriately, Midnight. Colby gave Nikki's backside a parting swat. "Now run a good race, kid."

Adrenaline pumped through Nikki's veins as the pony boy led her horse from the paddock in the pre-race parade. The bright lights, the colorful crowd, the excitement and tension of the moment were intoxicating. All those early years swept through her mind in a jumbled memory, the small-town quarter-horse races, the rodeos, the countless stalls she had mucked out, the exercise tracks. It had all led up to this moment.

One question clawed at her over and over. Will I be good enough?

Then she was in the narrow, padded stall of the starting gate, feeling the nervous energy of the powerful beast under her. There was a momentary sinking feeling in her stomach. Could she really control this charging monster when he exploded out of the starting gate? She was perched high on the saddle, her back straight. The strain on her knees and legs for the next two minutes would be tremendous.

The starting bell. The gate sprung open. "They're off!"

Afterward she remembered it in a blur. Colby's words echoing in her ear. "Let him take the lead early. He's got the stamina to hold it."

Mud flew in her face, blinding her goggles. A quick switch to a clean pair. Every muscle in her body strained to the breaking point. "Come on, you monster!" she sobbed. The horse needed no urging. Thoroughbred breeding and training had honed him to the edge of insanity. He had to run. He'd kill himself running if he had to. He'd gone berserk with the frantic need to run.

Nikki realized there was no more mud being thrown in her face. She had the lead. If Colby was right about the horse...

He was. Just as Colby predicted, the favorite, thrown out of kilter by the flying slop, was not running a good race. He never did break out of the pack. Nikki's Midnight crossed the finish line a length ahead of the nearest contender. Once she'd taken the lead, there had been no serious challenger.

There was the delirious, triumphant moment of victory, being in the winner's circle, having the reporters' cameras flash. She saw the jockey riding the favorite take off his helmet and throw it in the mud in disgust. Beaten by a woman!

Colby, grinning proudly, reached up to give her hand a squeeze.

A pony boy took the bridle, led her toward the paddock. She slid from the saddle, into a pair of strong arms that caught and held her. She felt herself pressed against a hard, masculine body. Shocked, she looked up into a pair of intense black eyes that sent a shiver down her spine.

"Congratulations, Nikki," said Jacques Trenchard. "Now let's go celebrate."

Chapter Six

With Jacques' arms holding her, the excitement of the race was temporarily blotted from her senses by a greater excitement.

For the past twenty-four hours, she had strained to block the disturbing chaos this man had brought to her emotions. She had forced herself to concentrate on the race. But now she could no longer avoid the devastating impact of his touch. Her body throbbed from the contact. His gaze plummeted to the depths of her being.

"What—what do you mean, celebrate?" she asked unsteadily.

He raised an eyebrow, his dark eyes twinkling. "Does horse racing give you an appetite? I thought we could have another dinner together. This time with more romantic surroundings than a horse barn."

Her eyes narrowed. "I don't know about that." She raised her chin. "You made me pretty mad last night."

He held up both hands in mock surrender. "Could we call a truce over a dinner for two?"

"I am starved," she admitted. "I haven't eaten a bite all day so I wouldn't be over my weight at the prerace weigh-in."

Jacques shook his head, his eyes showing concern. "You must be ready to faint."

She shrugged. "Some jockeys do starve themselves to the point of fainting to meet the weight requirements. But I'm not quite to that stage, yet."

"Nevertheless, we'd better get you to a thick, juicy steak promptly."

"Well..." She felt her mouth watering. Then suddenly, with his dark eyes looking at her so intensely, she became acutely self-conscious of her appearance. "But first I have to get cleaned up. That muddy track must have me looking like a mess."

"You look adorable, mud and all," Jacques said, not taking his eyes off her.

His steady gaze was robbing her knees of what little strength they had left. "I—I won't be long," she stammered. "Wait here." Then she fled to the women's dressing room. She was thankful that this was one of the more modern tracks that provided a dressing room with a shower for female jockeys.

She stared at her image in the dressing-room mirror. Her outfit, from the silken top to the pants stuffed into the tops of riding boots, were splattered with mud. "Girl, you are a mess!" Except for the clean area where her goggles had provided protection, her face was as muddy as her clothes. Her hair was a tangled disaster.

"This is going to take a complete overhaul," she muttered. It was suddenly very important to look her best for Jacques.

She scrubbed off the dirt of the track in a steaming shower, then toweled her skin to a glowing pink. She slipped into clean, fresh underthings, combed the tangles out of her hair and brushed it until it glowed with soft highlights. Some time was spent in applying delicate shades of makeup, a hint of eyeliner and eyeshadow, a brush of rouge.

Finally, she slipped on a pair of clean jeans that hugged her boyish curves and a hot-pink turtleneck knitted top, then pulled expensive, tooled-leather western boots on her feet. She gazed at her mirrored reflection doubtfully. "I look like a little ol' cowgirl." she muttered, suddenly wishing she had brought something more feminine. These were the kind of clothes she felt comfortable in around the horse barns and tracks. Besides, Brad had said he'd pick her up after the race and he liked to eat at a kicker hangout.

Brad!

"Oh, no, I forgot all about him," she said aloud, slapping her forehead. "Now what am I going to do?"

She'd just have to tell Jacques she might have made a previous date. But that was not the solution she preferred. Jacques Trenchard was the most disturbing man she had ever met. Warning bells and lights were going off inside her like a tilted pinball machine. Still, she was intrigued by him, fascinated, drawn to the danger with an overwhelming force.

She didn't actually have a date with Brad. They'd run around together so much they didn't make formal dates. Besides they were basically just *good* friends. Brad would show up and she'd go out with him. He'd said something about possibly being here tonight, taking it for granted that she'd go someplace with him after the race. Nikki thought he'd understand if she went off with Jacques instead.

With that decision out of the way, she gathered her courage and returned to where Jacques was waiting. Just looking at him took her breath away.

He turned, saw her and his face lit up with a glow that instantly warmed her. How feminine it made her feel to be looked at that way by such a devastating man!

"I—I hope you don't mind the jeans and boots. It's all I brought to the track."

"Of course I don't mind, Nikki," he replied, squeezing her hands warmly. "You look exquisite. Now I know just the place to go, where they serve thick steaks and crisp salads."

"Are you sure it's not too formal for the way I'm dressed?"

"It's casual, I assure you."

They started toward the parking area. Suddenly Brad Hall appeared in the crowd. "Hey, Nikki! I've been looking for you."

Uh-oh, she thought.

"Hi," he said, coming up to them. "Great race. I won forty bucks on you. Ready to go?"

He gave Jacques a curious look.

"Oh, Brad, I want you to meet Jacques Trenchard. Jacques, this is Brad Hall...an old friend."

"How do you do?" Jacques said.

There was a cold handshake as the two men sized each other up.

Nikki was struck by the difference between them. Brad, with his tousled blond hair, scuffed boots and sport shirt, looked very much a boy. Jacques was very much a man.

"Brad, I'm sorry. I wasn't sure if you'd show up. I told Jacques I'd go with him to get something to eat."

A sullen look crossed Brad's handsome young face. "Wha'd'ya mean, you didn't know if I'd show up? I thought I told you I'd pick you up after the race."

"Well, it wasn't definite," Nikki insisted.

There was a moment of strained silence. Now Brad was gazing at Jacques with open antagonism. "Okay, if that's how you feel about it," he said shortly. He turned and stalked off.

The awkward silence lingered as Jacques escorted Nikki to his car. He broke it, asking, "Your boyfriend?"

"Sort of."

Nikki was suddenly aware of an edge in Jacques' voice, a knotting of his jaw. He's jealous! she thought with a peculiar surge of delight. Up to now Jacques' cosmopolitan sophistication made her feel unsure and naive. The realization that she had the power to make him jealous gave her a base of self-assurance she hadn't had before. Making the most of the situation, she added, "Brad and I go back a long way."

She stole a glance at Jacques to measure the effect of her words and saw, to her amused delight, the knotting of his jaw again.

He took her to an informal place where some of the racetrack crowd hung out. It had a country-western flavor, with steer horns on the mirror behind the bar and a country-western band. A lot of people recognized Nikki. Tonight she was a celebrity.

"Hey, Nikki. Great race!"

"Congratulations, girl. Your picture is going to make the front page of the sports section tomorrow."

Nikki signed several autographs. She couldn't remember when she'd been so happy.

Jacques watched it all with a look of amused tolerance.

When they regained some privacy at a secluded booth, Nikki couldn't keep from having her moment of triumph. "Well, Mr. Male Chauvinist, do you still think only men can jockey thoroughbreds?"

His hearty, infectious laughter put her in a good mood. "Nikki, you are an outstanding horsewoman. Out there on the track tonight, you were absolutely superb. I laughed when the jockey on the favorite threw his helmet in the mud after the race. He looked so humiliated!"

She grinned. "That was pretty funny," she agreed.

"I still think it's too dangerous for a woman, though," he insisted. "Call me an old-fashioned male chauvinist if you wish, horse racing should be a man's job."

Nikki was in too good a mood to be angry. She just wrinkled her nose at him and said, "Well, Mr. He-man, someday I'll get you out on a racetrack and run circles around you."

Her joyful mood grew as the evening progressed. She felt deliriously happy. Everything was funny. The world was a delightful place.

She was in a state of euphoria. Part of it was winning her first race. But mostly it was being with Jacques. She became intoxicated with being with Jacques. His glance heightened her own awareness of herself. His touch sent electric currents through her body.

There was so much for them to talk about, so much she wanted to hear him say, so much she had to say to him. She hadn't dreamed just being with a man, hearing his voice, watching his hands move as he lit a cigarette or toyed with his glass, could have such meaning. Time was suspended. Space ceased to exist. They were in their own world, excluding the sounds and movement around them. They touched with their eyes, with their words, with their fingers.

She was filled with joy. Her heart was overflowing. Her whole being sang with delight. Her body throbbed with happiness.

In a dreamlike sequence, the evening slipped away and then they were in Jacques' car, driving on the freeways, along winding, narrow country roads to the neat white fences curving over the rolling hillsides of Elmhurst Farms.

In the driveway, when Jacques parked in the deep shadows under the great elms, Nikki melted into his arms. Jacques' lips touched hers in their first kiss. It was a moment that would forever be frozen in time. Their lives would go on, but that breathless instant of joy would somehow continue in a dimension all its own, as eternal as the twinkling stars in the velvet sky and the moonlight bathing the Kentucky hillsides with silver.

Nikki felt her mouth catch fire from Jacques's lips. He whispered her name against her lips and kissed her again and again, each kiss growing more hungry than the one before, and she gave of herself, eager to satisfy that hunger.

His lips trailed a fiery pattern down her cheek to the soft hollow of her throat. Her eyes were closed, her head rested on the seat cushion. Her fingers caressed his cheeks, threaded through the luxurious thickness of his dark hair. His fingers were touching the buttons of her shirt.

Her body was weak with desire. There was no strength in her muscles to resist. She felt the coolness of the night air on her bare skin as the buttons of her shirt slipped open. Then coolness turned to burning flame as his lips sought the secret, delicate curves of her bosom.

"Jacques...Jacques..." she whispered, breathing hard.

From a distance, she heard him speaking her name. She opened bemused eyes, and was held by the passion of his gaze. "Nikki, I have never had a woman affect me like this. I adore you, my darling, precious Nikki!"

"This...this is crazy," she whispered, shaking her head slowly. "I just met you yesterday. Things like this don't happen."

"Yes they do," he murmured, gazing at her and gently kissing her fingertips. "Nikki, I must see you again."

A little shiver ran through her. She was in the grip of such overpowering emotions that she was frightened. Seeing him again...what would it mean?

"I—I don't know, Jacques," she stammered, and she fled into the house.

But he called the next day and she went with him again. She craved his kisses with an intensity that overwhelmed her.

For the first time since she could remember, her mind was filled with something besides horses. She went through her daily routine in a fog, unable to concentrate. The man has cast some kind of spell over me, she thought with a kind of panic.

"What's eating you, Nikki?" her father asked in exasperation one day after she'd galloped a horse on the exercise track. "You aren't listening to a word I say. How do you expect to learn anything?"

"I'm sorry, Dad. I was listening."

"No you weren't, your mind was a thousand miles away. It's that French fellah you've been running around with, isn't it? I've never seen you moon around like this over any of the local young stallions."

Nikki's face reddened. "I—I do like Jacques...."

"I don't think 'like' is a strong enough word." He looked at her, his eyes filled with concern. Clumsily, he clasped her hand. "Honey, I got kinda late being a daddy to you. Heck, I wasn't a daddy at all when you were a little girl. You grew up without any help from me. And now you're already a grown woman. I don't have much say in how you live your life. Just be careful, okay? More than one woman has gone daft over some guy and had her heart broken. You reckon this French aristocrat of yours has marriage in mind?''

Her embarrassment increased. "Daddy, I don't know.''

"Right now, you're all wrapped up in this man," her father said, continuing to look worried. "He's all you can think about. But I know you, Nikki. You have horse racing in your blood. In the long run, nothing is going to change that.''

"Why, nothing would!'' she exclaimed.

"Don't be too sure, honey. If your man is serious enough to want to marry you, it could change everything. He's no racetrack Johnny. That boy has the blue blood of French aristocracy coursing through his veins. He's a thoroughbred, like the string of horses he owns. He'd want you to go back to France with him, become a regular lady. He'd have you jet hopping from Swiss chalets to Greek yachts. He wouldn't put up with a wife jock making the racetrack circuit.''

"Dad—''

"No, hear me out, honey, then you do what you want. I've got nothin' against you marrying rich and joining the country-club set. Fact is, in a way I'd be relived. I wouldn't have to lie awake nights, worrying about you bustin' your sweet neck on some dirt track or getting trampled into the mud. I never had it in my heart for you to become a jockey. I just saw there was nothing I could do to stop you, so I made up my mind to teach you how to be the best jockey on the tracks, to have the know-how to win and the knowledge to keep from gettin' hurt if possible. But now you've tasted what it's like to win a race. That horse love you've got in your blood isn't going to go away so easily. You might put it out of your mind for a while with the glamour of getting married and all. But somewhere down the line it's going to crop up and eat at you till you won't be able to stand it.''

Nikki found her father's warning profoundly disturbing. She worked harder than ever, galloping horses furiously on the exercise track, riding until she was exhausted.

To avoid seeing Jacques one evening, she phoned Brad Hall. He drove over in his latest sports car and they went for a wild drive through the country. Nikki rode with the top down, welcoming the wind whipping her face and hair.

"Let's stop at the country club," she suggested.

They played a hard game of tennis under the light, then went for a swim in the club pool. "Race you!" Nikki shouted. They swam two laps, then she dragged herself up on the side of the pool, laughing when she caught her breath.

"What's got into you tonight?" Brad demanded, gulping air into his straining lungs as he clambered up on the pool beside her. "You haven't slowed down since we left home."

"We're having fun, aren't we?"

"Sure."

"I always have fun with you, Brad. I want life to go on like this, chasing around, having fun, riding horses, winning horse races."

He gave her a curious look. "What's eating you, Nikki? You sound so intense."

"Nothing's eating me. I don't know what you're talking about. Brad, I want a drink."

"Okay. Let's get dressed and I'll meet you at the bar."

Several cocktails later, they headed for home. With the wind whipping through her hair, Nikki was singing a ribald racetrack song at the top of her lungs.

Several hours before that, Jacques had arrived at Elmhurst Farms. Colby Cameron had greeted him with a friendly handshake. "I came to pick up Nikki," Jacques explained. "Is she ready?"

Colby cleared his throat. "Well, Jacques," he said, "I'm afraid she's already left."

Jacques stared at Nikki's father, his face coloring. "I don't understand. I was planning on spending the evening with her."

Colby shrugged. "Nikki," he said, "can be kind of unpredictable."

Jacques scowled. "But I thought she knew I was coming over—"

Colby made a helpless gesture. "My friend, I'm her father, but Nikki is a grown woman...."

Jacques's scowl deepened. "Did she leave with anyone?"

"I saw her drive off with Brad Hall."

A wave of blind fury swept through Jacques, along with a feeling of emptiness in the pit of his stomach. Brad Hall again! Nikki's words came back to torment him. *Brad and I go back a long way.*

What was the implication of that? Were they lovers?

The thought of Nikki somewhere in Brad Hall's arms, of Brad kissing her, undressing her, making love to her, seared through Jacques like a red-hot branding iron. The agony was unbearable.

Colby saw the anguish in Jacques's eyes. "Don't be too hard on her, son," Colby said gently. "Nikki's going through a tough time right now. I think she cares about you, but she also cares about horse racing. It's her whole life. She's at war with herself over that."

She can't think that much about me if she's out with another man, Jacques thought.

"Come on in," Colby suggested. "I've got some choice Kentucky sour mash. We'll have a drink, then I'll take you on a tour of our stables, show you some of the best horseflesh in the state."

Jacques appreciated the trainer's effort to get his mind off his mental anguish, but nothing was going to alleviate his burning jealousy.

After a tour of the stables, Jacques went back out to his car to wait for Nikki. He was grimly determined to wait if it took all night. He had to have this matter resolved.

It was near dawn when Nikki and Brad pulled into the winding driveway of Elmhurst Farms. Nikki saw a low-slung foreign sports car parked near the house. A tall, lean, broad-shouldered figure was leaning against it. He flicked a lighter to his cigarette and the glow touched the dark, angry countenance of Jacques Trenchard.

"Uh-oh," Nikki murmured.

"What's he doing here?" Brad demanded.

"I think I stood him up tonight," Nikki admitted.

"So what?" Brad scowled. "Maybe he'll get the message and leave."

Brad whipped his car to a stop beside Jacques, slinging gravel. Nikki jumped out. "Hi, Jacques," she said breezily.

He flicked his cigarette to the ground. His dark eyes blazed with fury. "I believe we had a date tonight?"

"It wasn't definite," she said, tossing her head. "I said I'd think about it."

His scowl darkened. "Nikki, you've been drinking."

"Uh-huh. A bunch." She giggled.

Brad got out of his car and moved around to join them. "Nikki's with me tonight. Why don't you beat it?"

Jacques looked at Brad as if murder were on his mind. "I want to have a word with Nikki."

"You've had a word. Now go home."

Ignoring him, Jacques took Nikki's arm. "Let's go in the house and get you some coffee," he said. "I want to talk to you."

Brad grabbed Jacques' arm. "I said beat it, buster."

A look crossed Jacques's face that made Nikki's blood turn cold. Nervously she said, "Brad, maybe it would be better if you'd leave. I had a great time tonight. I'll call you tomorrow...."

"No way. I'm going to teach this guy a lesson."

"I don't want to fight with you, Brad. Do what Nikki said and go home."

"You're the one who's leaving," Brad fumed. "In an ambulance—"

With a look of resignation, Jacques grabbed Brad and dumped him in his car. He leaned over and turned the key, starting the motor. "Now go home," he ordered.

Brad sat there for a moment, his hair tumbled over his handsome young face. Sobering rapidly, he realized he was no match for Jacques. He gave Jacques a look of bitter hatred, then swung the steering wheel and dug out, slinging gravel in all directions.

Nikki was sobbing with fury. "You beast!" She swung her hand back as if to slap him, but he ducked, catching her wrist in midair. He grabbed her other hand and held on with all his might as she struggled furiously.

"You little wildcat!" He laughed, surprised at how strong she was.

"Let me go!" she demanded.

"What, and let you make a punching bag out of me?"

"He had just as much business being here as you. What gives the right to chase my boyfriends out of my yard?"

There was a moment of heavy silence. Jacques was staring at Nikki with a dark, smoldering expression. "Is Brad your boyfriend?" he asked in a low, strained voice.

Nikki raised her chin defiantly. "Yes. We've run around together since we were kids. We're practically engaged."

Again the deadly silence. An expression of pain wrenched across Jacques's face. A maelstrom of emotions were churning through his eyes, jealousy, hurt, fury.

He swallowed hard and asked words that tasted like acid. "Is he your lover?"

Nikki shrugged defiantly. "I don't think that's any of your business."

Still holding her arms, he shook her. "Yes, it is my business!" he raged. "What's the matter with you, you little fool? Can't you see I'm in love with you ? The way we've been together the last few nights...the way you've kissed me. How could you do that and go to another man? I can't believe you're that kind of woman!"

He held her, still struggling, closer to him, held her tightly until gradually her struggling subsided and she grew limp in the strength of his arms.

The fight drained out of her, Nikki started crying. "Please leave me alone. I'm—I'm all mixed up."

He held her closer, murmuring in her hair.

"No, Jacques," she sobbed, turning her face away.

"Nikki, look at me."

"No!"

Gently he put his finger under her chin, forced her streaming eyes to gaze up at him.

There was a long moment. All the violent rebellion that had stormed through Nikki that night became fragmented. She felt her knees growing weak.

"No, Jacques.... No..." she whimpered.

But he drew her closer. She felt the iron bands of his arms, the hard masculine contours of his body. Against her will, she melted into his embrace.

He held her like that for a long moment, warming her body with his. Then he kissed her savagely. All his raging emotion of the evening was released in the kiss. It was searching, demanding, almost cruel. Above all, it was furiously passionate.

At first her mouth was stiff and then it relaxed and grew hungry under his. Her body pressed harder against his, wanting to be closer...closer....

"Nikki," he whispered in her hair, "why do you behave like this? Why do you go off on a wild spree with Brad? You must care for me or you couldn't respond to me like this."

"I don't want to get involved with you, Jacques!" she cried. "My future is all planned. I'm a professional jockey. I've done very well in my first races. They've granted my license. I'm going to be a famous jockey...."

"What are you trying to prove, Nikki?"

"It's not a matter of proving anything. Don't you understand? Horses are my life. Riding is my life. It's the only time I feel totally alive, when I'm on a thoroughbred that's running his heart out for me. There's no place in my life for you, for marriage...."

"I don't believe that," he said, gazing deeply into her eyes. "I think you were out with Brad tonight, chasing around the country, playing too hard, drinking too much, because you're trying to run away from your feelings about me. Tell me that's the truth."

Desperately, Nikki put her hands over her ears. "I won't listen!"

"Look at me," he ordered, grasping her face in his hands, forcing her eyes to meet his. "Tell me you are not in love with me."

She sobbed, "Jacques, don't do this to me."

"Tell me!"

"No!"

"You do love me, Nikki," he said hoarsely. "You want me as much as I want you. And that's a fact. You're trying to deny it, to run away from it, but you can't—"

Again he kissed her, a kiss that drained every shred of her resistance. She gasped for breath as passion became a tidal wave.

"Oh, Jacques, what am I going to do about you?" she moaned.

"I'll tell you what you're going to do."

He stripped her blouse from her shoulder. Her head fell back. Weakly, she fell against his car. His kisses rained a trail of fire over her throat, the soft, shadowy hollow of her shoulder.

Her knees could no longer hold her. "Nikki... Nikki," Jacques whispered, his breath hoarse in his throat.

He scooped her up in strong arms and carried her to the nearest barn, laid her gently on a pile of loose hay. His hands moved over her back, under the blouse, opened the clasps of her bra. He captured her leg between his. Her body burned with desire. Her hips moved, grinding herself against him. He opened her blouse, burying his face in the fragrant, yielding mounds of her bosom.

"Nikki, I want you...I want you...."

She was out of her mind with passion that poured like molten liquid through her veins. "Yes..." she sobbed. "Yes."

All of her resistance had been swept away. Her mind was no longer functioning on a rational level. She was his for the taking.

But with a sudden gentleness, he said, "Not now, my darling. Not here, in a horse barn. What I feel for you is so much more than that. Marry me, Nikki. Stop fighting it. Stop fighting me. You're wearing yourself out fighting it. Destiny meant for us to be together forever. Marry me, Nikki. Marry me. Be my wife. We'll be married in a beautiful cathedral before all the world. We'll be together, sleep together, have children together. Say yes, my sweet, adorable Nikki. Please say yes, and I'll see that the whole world is spread at your feet. You won't regret it, I promise."

A week later, Jacques placed a large diamond on her finger.

Nikki had to deal with an emotional storm when the news reached Brad Hall. He called her, drunk and sobbing. "How can you do something this dumb, Nikki? It's always been you and me, ever since high school. You were going to marry me...."

"Brad, we never made definite plans—"

"Maybe we never set an exact date, but it was understood...."

Nikki tried to be as gentle and patient as was humanly possible. She had always been very fond of Brad, though she had never experienced the blinding, all-consuming passion with Brad that Jacques could arouse in her. With Brad, she felt more of the tenderness she would toward a dear brother. Nevertheless, she felt a deep responsibility not to hurt him.

"Brad, honey, you're my very best friend, you know that. We've had so much fun together all these years. But I just never felt that way about you. Can't we stay good friends and always remember the good times we had?"

"You're making a mistake!" Brad said heatedly. "This guy swept you off your feet with his smooth continental line. The marriage isn't going to last. You'll be back. And I'll be here waiting when you do—"

For a moment, Nikki felt a chilling shadow fall over her happiness. Had Brad uttered some kind of frightening prophecy?

Then she reminded herself that it was the liquor and hurt feelings talking. She could tell that Brad was sincerely broken up over her engagement to Jacques. She desperately wished there were something she could do to ease his pain, but in the final analysis it was something he had to deal with. Brad wasn't accustomed to disappointments. His family had spoiled him. She supposed this was the first real heartbreak he had known, though she wasn't sure if he truly cared that much about her or if it was his male pride that was suffering.

In any case, she felt sure he would survive. She reassured herself that in a few months he'd be out making the racetrack, country-club circuit with a brand-new girlfriend and would forget all about Nikki Cameron.

By the end of the month, she was Mrs. Jacques Trenchard. They spent their honeymoon in France.

It was the beginning of a very short and stormy marriage.

Chapter Seven

It was a Paris honeymoon, a romantic setting from a Hemingway novel.

Jacques had said, "The Lotti. Yes, I'll reserve a suite at the Lotti before we fly out of New York. It's not a tourist trap; a hotel for the discerning, for us. The restaurant may strike you as a corridor from the lobby into the bar, but it's always full and you'll love the pâté maison de grives, the mignon de veau, when we go down to dine. At the Lotti the room service is superb and the beds are excellently large...."

"So you're really going to do it," André Broussard had exclaimed. After meeting Nikki, he understood. "She's an exciting, seductive combination of honey nectar and fiery spice. A worthy match for you, my stubborn friend. You have my blessing and my congratulations on one condition." He clapped his friend on the shoulder. "I must be best man at the wedding and first to kiss the bride!"

"Of course you'll be best man, *mon ami*!" Jacques agreed.

And so he was at the ceremony in one of the finest cathedrals in all France....

Then...later, in their honeymoon bed. "Yes, Jacques! Oh, yes!" Nikki's murmuring lips felt moistly hot, swollen with passion. Her breasts strained to lift to him. She burned with passion, drowned in waves of desire. She didn't care. "Take me, Jacques...take me and never let me go...."

A honeymoon in Paris. What could be more romantic?

On their honeymoon bed, he was an image of lean, naked virility reaching out for her as she came from the bath, pink, steamy, eager, as hungry for him as he for her.

"Stand a moment," he whispered, and she stood, shivery with the impact of his desire as his eyes swept her from head to toe like tongues of fire.

"Nikki, Nikki," he said hoarsely. "Are you real, or a nymph from some hidden glen in the forests of the Argonne? Dare I believe you are real?"

"Dare," she whispered thickly, sinking down beside him. Her hands moved over him in intimate caresses. "Is that real?" she asked huskily. She could sense the latent power in the lean cords of his muscles, the wiriness that could ripple and explode into bone-crushing strength. The knowledge made her tremble.

But his first touches of exploration were gentle, almost tentative, as if he had savored the certainty of this moment too long to have it over quickly.

She longed for the moment to last as well, touching his lips at first softly, letting her fingers trace the line of his cheek, his shoulder, the short, dark, curly hairs on his chest.

He'd drawn the draperies of the tall windows not quite closed and a soft brush of pearl glow touched the room from the lights of Paris. Touching, caressing, they held back in unspoken understanding, letting desire build into explosive anticipation. Then when they could bear it no longer, the meeting of their lips was savage.

His pent-up power was a raging storm, taking command of her. She moaned in pleasure. Her arms were about him, her nails digging into his back.

She was being borne up into sensation where space and time ceased to exist, where pleasure soared to heights that brought a small outcry from her.

Later, lying liquidly spent, swathed with a sense of repletion, dewy with the perspiration of their exertions, she tenderly stroked the fine dark hair pillowed against her shoulder.

"Jacques," she whispered. "I do love you so very, very much. You know something?"

"What?" He didn't lift his head, his lips moving against the softness of her neck.

"You knew all along. You were right. We were born for each other."

"Very right, darling," he said with a sleepy smile.

Her contentment matched his. Sprawled together, limbs carelessly entwined, she let herself drift into soft, depthless slumber.

She awoke the next morning slowly, dreamily, wanting to stretch and purr like a kitten. Her palm slid across the sheet, rumpled and hinting at the masculine smell of him. She sat up, alone. "Jacques?"

He didn't respond. The door of the bathroom was open. She didn't hear him moving elsewhere in the suite. She was alone in the subtle elegance of the room with its aura of tradition and ageless refinement.

A top sheet was drawn over her and she saw her robe where he'd folded it and placed it neatly on the bedside stand.

Lying atop the robe was a note he'd left her. She frowned, but the frown turned to a smile by the time she had finished reading the note:

Darling, you were angelically lovely in sleep with that satisfied little smile on your face. I couldn't bear to disturb you, much as I wanted to take a bite of you. I'm off to that bit of business I mentioned. I've delayed it through the trip and your putting the velvet ring of marriage through my joyous nose. But I simply can't keep Louden Ltd. waiting any longer or they'll sign with a competitor. We are trying to sell them a parcel of land near Cherbourg where they'll build a plant to turn out molded hulls for their motorboats. Unfortunately, a wily Belgian has been trying to lure them to the vicinity of Antwerp. I really should close the deal while I am winning. Then I'll pick you up a diamond necklace with part of the profit! Meantime, be assured that the Lotti staff knows how to treat royalty, else it wouldn't have been the lifetime choice in Paris of the Duke of Westminster. I may be tied up for several hours, but you're in a city with no end of sight-seeing and exploration. Just don't taxi yourself 10 miles out to the Maisons Lafitte; I absolutely must be at your side when you first see thoroughbreds racing on French soil! I'll either have the barristers and cartelists out of the way in time to pick you up for dinner, or Louden Ltd. can go to Antwerp or some unmentionable place.

He'd signed the note with a flourishing "J."

Her eyes fondled the words dashed off in his second language. How many languages could he manage? She knew he was proficient in German and Spanish as well. The slight accent he had in English only added to his cosmopolitan charm.

One day he might be in Keeneland bidding on a yearling, the next driving a hard bargain in Europe with an international conglomerate.

Her throat felt suddenly dry with the realization that she was married to a stranger. Or more accurately, a stranger from a different world. She'd accepted the fact that they were from different worlds, but she had been too swept off her feet to give it much deep thought. It was one thing to mention to yourself that the sun was hot; it was quite another to realize that if you drowsed off on a beach blanket, you might awaken a couple of hours later red and blistered, feeling as if you'd been sizzled on a skewer.

Now in the quiet of the lovely July morning, the bricks and mortar began to sink in. She was in Paris, twenty years old, married to a French industrialist and aristocrat. She was a girl from Kentucky whose background began to feel very shaky. A sense of being alone in deep waters started to assail her. Resolutely she curbed it as she would command a fractious stallion into the starting gate.

Jacques had seen her in her own milieu, from mud-splattered riding outfit to evening gowns at the great house at Elmhurst. His experience and worldly eyes had taken it all in, who she was, where she came from. He was aware that she had polish and style, a refinement taught her by Elvira and exposure to the country-club set, but he'd also heard her racetrack expletives blister the air. He had no doubt that she could lay an antagonistic jockey out cold with a vicious left hook if it came to that. Yet of all the women he could have—the movie starlets, the cream of European society—he had chosen her. Why? It was not a question she could answer. Love did not lend itself to mathematical formulas or cold logic.

The point was, she was now Mrs. Nikki Cameron Trenchard—or, more accurately, Madame Nikki Cameron Trenchard. That was the bottom line. That knowledge filled her with exultation. She would refuse to even consider the nagging, shadowy anxieties.

Her self-confidence renewed, Nikki tasted the day with fresh excitement, ready to sample Paris, jewel city of the world....

"In Paris," Jacques had instructed her, "if you ever take a wrong turn and get lost, there is an essential phrase you should know, *Y a-t-il quelqu'un qui parle anglais?* Someone will invariably respond, 'Yes, mademoiselle, I speak English. How may I assist?' If she's female, you will have made a friend. If male, he'll prove to you that chivalry isn't at all dead. You'll find France the most gracious of hostesses."

Okay, Nikki thought as she sallied out to breakfast. I'll give the hostess her chance!

With a guidebook and pocket English-French vocabulary of handy phrases, Nikki was off on her day as a tourist. And when finally at eight that evening she was a lovely young French wife seated across a candlelit dinner table from a D'Artagnan husband a few years her senior, her eyes were sparkling as if the long span of hours had refreshed rather than tired her.

"Jacques, it's so...so ageless...so mellowed by time, yet so eager for tomorrow."

His eyes smiled at her bubbling enthusiasm. "Where did you start, darling?"

She wrinkled her nose. "At the center, of course, the Île de la Cité, that wonderful boat-shaped island in the Seine where the pioneers set up their huts two hundred years before Christ. Oh, Jacques, the history is overwhelming. In America, everything is so new. We think of history in terms of hundreds of years. Here, it's more like thousands! I could almost hear the tramp of Roman legions, the Celts, the Visigoths. All the battles, the plagues of the Middle Ages, the Nazi occupation, and yet, through it all, Paris never lost the essence of herself, the love of art, science, beauty."

"How well put. You have the soul of a poet, my darling wife."

Seeing her dressed in the latest Paris fashions, her face aglow, her hair styled by a beautician recommended by the hotel, Jacques could not summon enough imagination to picture her coming off a racetrack, mud-splattered and sweaty, telling an offending male jockey in salty racetrack language what she though of his crowding her into the rail!

"Tell me what else you saw, Nikki."

"I was a shameless gawker, a typical tourist. What did I see? It's a jumble in my mind, the Tuileries, the elegant Place Vendôme, the Ritz, just a glimpse of the Louvre, where I could spend a week looking at art treasures I've only read about."

"Your day," Jacques said, laughing, "has worn me out just hearing about it. You covered more territory in a day than most Frenchmen could in a week. But that's how you Americans do things. Always in a rush, as if you must somehow cram two lifetimes into one."

He motioned to the waiter that he would pour the wine himself.

Nikki went on, a trifle breathlessly, "And all too suddenly I had to hurry back to seven rue de Gastiglione to drive my husband to distraction with chatter about my day."

"You drive me to distraction," he said, his dark eyes smoldering in a manner that suddenly took her breath away, "but not by your chatter."

She gazed at him shamelessly. Somehow, in Paris, it seemed quite all right to look at your husband with unmasked passion. She drank in the sight of his strong hands toying with a wineglass, his eyes, his hair, the smooth olive complexion. She caught the faint fragrance of his after-shave lotion. Above all, she became pulsatingly aware of his magnetism...its pull on her senses, on her body...the sweet yearning that awoke in her and quickly became a throbbing desire.

With an impulsive brazenness that surprised her, she touched his leg under the table, sliding her palm up his thigh. A flush crept to his throat as his eyes grew smoky. "Keep that up," he said thickly, "and we'll never get past the first course."

"Is it really so important?" she asked huskily.

He shook his head slowly, drenching her with his gaze. He summoned the head waiter. "We've decided to have a later dinner," he said.

Then they were in the elevator. They were in their room. With the door barely closed, their clothes were strewn on the floor.

"I feel like a naughty Parisian streetwalker," Nikki said with a grin. She felt abandoned in a mood of wickedness as Jacques crushed her in his arms.

She pressed her body to his eagerly. "I don't know what's gotten into me."

"It's Paris. The city of lovers," he said. "It gets in your blood."

"It must," she gasped. "My blood feels overheated. But it's not Paris...it's you...you, my husband. I can't seem to get enough of you...."

Later, spent and happy, she rested on her elbows, gazing down at his face. "Tell me about yourself, Jacques. About your family. Sometimes I think I hardly know you. What were you like as a little boy?"

"The usual. I climbed trees, played hooky from school, threw rocks in the river, shot out a window-pane with my BB gun."

They both laughed. "Not so different from an American boy. Did you ride horses?"

"Oh, yes. My family always had horses. Trenchard is a very old French name, going back to the days of the Normans and the Saxons. We have been a family of soldiers, land owners, capitalists. The usual collection of heroes and villains. During the French Revolution, the guillotine put an untimely end to some aristocratic members of the family, but others escaped to serve proudly under Napoleon. More recently, my great-grandfather died on a horse in the early months of World War One before machine guns convinced us that a modern war could no longer be fought with the cavalry. My grandfather fought the Nazis from a tank. My father rebuilt the family business, which I have now taken over. So...you have the story of my life. But please. Keep chattering about your day, Nikki. France has put her seal on you with a kiss, I think. And your talk reminds me that there is a Paris where I should pause and look afresh. Living in a land, you take it for granted—like the magnitude and endless contrast of America from the hustle of New York to the rustic beauty of your Kentucky bluegrass region."

For just a second, Nikki felt a stab of homesickness. She brushed it aside with a question about a yearling named New Diamond that Jacques had purchased from the Elmhurst Farms.

"Speaking of horses, when do I see New Diamond's French home?"

"In a day or so." He laughed. Then he suggested, "Are you ready to go back to the dining room for the meal that was so delightfully interrupted?"

"Yes indeed. Lovemaking, I find, gives me an appetite." Then, with a sudden blush, she said, "Do you think the maître d' will...will—"

"Suspect our reason for so impetuously leaving his dining room? He's a Frenchman, isn't he? I would be disappointed if he didn't."

"Oh, no!" she said, pressing her palms to her hot cheeks. "How can I face the man?"

"Proudly, of course! This is the city of lovers, my dear. He will very likely greet us with an envious smile and then proceed to present us with a bottle of fine champagne, compliments of the house!"

"You're all rascals, you know that? Now be a good husband and help me get this dress zipped up the back!"

Jacques was right about the twinkling smile from the maître d' and the complimentary champagne. After Nikki had survived that embarrassment and they were seated again at their table, she exclaimed with a stab of guilt, "Here I've been rattling on about my day of sightseeing and I haven't asked you a single word about the business you are involved in. Forgive me for not asking first thing."

He chuckled. "If you had, I would have thought la belle France was losing her grip." He touched the heavy while linen napkin to his lips. "I'm proud to report, my dear, that I returned to France in the nick of time. The potbellied little Belgian is probably right now having his

Pernod and hating me. But that reminds me. I believe I made a bargain with you.''

"A bargain?'' she asked, her eyes widening.

"You've forgotten already?'' His eyes twinkled. "I believe something was said about a diamond necklace if my business deal came off a success.''

With that, he drew a velvet case from his inner coat pocket and placed it on the white linen tablecloth beside her wineglass. Eyes wide as saucers, fingers trembling, Nikki picked it up. Slowly she opened the case for a peek inside. She gasped. True to his word, it was a diamond necklace, ablaze with fire. She lifted it to her throat, speechless, knowing it must have cost more than a twenty-to-one horse could have earned a heavy bettor by coming in first.

"Oh, Jacques, it's too much! You take it back.''

"You don't like it?''

"Of course I like it! What woman in her right mind wouldn't be ecstatic? It's the most beautiful thing I've ever seen. But how can you afford such extravagance?''

He smiled tolerantly. "You are not exactly married to a poor man, Nikki, my darling. And the deal I closed this morning made the necklace quite affordable, I assure you. My only concern is whether you like it.''

"Yes, Jacques. Yes, yes, yes! I love it. Dare I put it on now?''

"Why not?''

"I won't get mugged?''

Jacques threw his head back in one of his hearty spells of uninhibited laughter. "Nikki, I promise you that you won't get mugged. This hotel is famous for its security.''

"Then I will wear it," she said, reaching to the back of her neck to close the fastener. "There. How do I look?"

"Fabulous. Like a princess."

"It makes me feel wicked all over again."

"Perhaps," he suggested, a mischievous glint in his eye, "you'll model it for me tonight in our room...just the necklace."

"Nothing else?"

He grinned. "Perhaps a pair of high heels."

"You," she said severely, "are a very wicked minded man. I'll have to think about it." Her eyes were full of teasing promise when she spoke. "Now tell me about the yearlings."

"I assure you that New Diamond is happily grazing in pastures nearly as sweet as Kentucky bluegrass. While she's making yearling friends, I want to see Paris through your eyes, Montmartre, Notre Dame, the Eiffel Tower. And I'll show you some of the byways, Lipp on Saint-Germain, a favorite haunt of politicians, writers, film people, the auction at Drouot's, Trilby's on rue Franklin, a small bookshop with the finest personal service in the world.

"Then," he went on, "we'll head south and try not to see what commercial tourism has done to some of the locations along the Riviera. The older generation would tell you that the weather in the south of France, land of the fabled villas, luxury hotels, stately white-sailed yachts rocking in picturebook harbors, has deteriorated steadily for the past forty to fifty years. The mistral, the wind from the north, seems to occur far too frequently. A foot of snow all the way from Toulon to

Menton would have been incredible back when Hemingway, Scott Fitzgerald and Cole Porter were showing France what their breed of Americans was all about. But we'll wander down to Les Oliviers and I'll treat you to a dinner at a delightful outdoor restaurant where a tree grows oranges and lemons at the same time, thanks to some grafting by a genius. But first, I see the waiter is about to serve the escargot."

"Yes," Nikki said with some trepidation, relying on Jacques' assurance that if she liked oysters on the half-shell, which she did, she would fall addict after her first escargot experience. She was so excited over the necklace and the prospect of a sight-seeing tour of Paris and southern France that the extravagant French meal was almost wasted on her; she was hardly aware of what she was eating.

The next several days rushed by Nikki, giving her a breathless feeling of having no more substance than a rainbow. When Jacques had used the word "wander," he seemed to have meant it. He would change the direction of the Audi station wagon as if on a whim simply because he suddenly thought of some little byway sight he wanted her to see.

The Loire valley, she quickly decided, was like no other place on earth. The placid river wended across central France through rich and gently rolling countryside. It breathed history through its Renaissance castles, its picturesque villages, the stained glass from the twelfth century in a cavernous cathedral. The sun kissed the richness of a landscape of neat farms that reflected the industriousness of a friendly people. Grapes grew along the gentle slopes of the riverside, yielding such treasures as Coulée-de-Serrant, Coteaux de Layon, adaptable Vouvray. Also for the table were delights that were presented to Nikki in dizzying array, lark pies, crow soup, the savory butter sauce of Anjou, port and goose dishes, stuffed fish of Anjou, sausages from Gatinais, poached eggs in Vouvray jelly from the Touraine, wild game delicacies cooked in ways beyond Nikki's imagining.

It was a period of careless, carefree existence. The Audi was loaded with luggage, sleeping bags, food containers. If they stopped for a gaggle of geese crossing a narrow back road, Jacques might decide that the shady glen off to the left was the ideal place to spread a lunch and promptly jounce the car in that direction.

But if the days were a process of mind-boggling discovery and education, the nights were experiences Nikki had never fantasized. They stopped at village inns, hotels in serene, secluded nooks in the countryside where sleeping bags could be spread beneath the stars. They made love in gentle touches and in breathless body-to-body clashes, in slumbrous ease and in wild impatience. He awakened a passion and fulfillment that she never dreamed could exist.

And at last he was saying: "When we top the next rise you will see it. Château Trenchard, New Diamond's present home. But I warn you, it's not nearly as imposing as the appellation might suggest. The château happens to be a rambling old farmhouse and the lands are not as extensive as those at Elmhurst."

She sat straight up in the seat, straining for her first look. Momentarily her mind erased reflections of the delightful wandering that had taken them as far south as out-of-the-way auberges on the Moyenne Corniche.

The station wagon suddenly faltered on the narrow access road.

"Oh, damn!" Jacques said.

Then she saw the tug in his lips, the boyish glint in his eyes.

"You tease," she cried.

He laughed, then reached for the ignition as her sandaled foot slammed down on the accelerator. The Audi surged forward, causing him to grab the steering wheel tighter. "Woman, do you want to wreck us?" he roared.

"I want to see the Château Trenchard, you horrible man."

Their shoulders fell against each other while their laughter mingled, ringing out, silly, wonderful, like two kids.

Then the long view spread before her and Jacques eased the car to a halt on the summit of the gentle rise. Far, far in the distance, miles away, the bright sunlight reflected a silver ribbon, the river Loire. From horizon to horizon, the river made a gentle bend like a maternally protecting arm. Between the viewpoint and the river on the horizon to the north, the landscape was beyond the scope of picture postcard.

The farms were neat checkerboard squares marked by narrow roads, hedgerows, fences. They lay like manicured models—green fields, pastures, vineyards, acres cultivated in neat rows. On a hillside far away moved flecks of white, a herd of sheep. Etched on a low tableland a stallion stood guard over a harem of mares. In contrast to the old-world essence, the timeliness of it, motor traffic rushed with twentieth-century speed along a distant highway linking teeming, bustling cities where a Coke or even the Colonel's fried chicken might be had.

"Which is yours, Jacques?" Nikki asked as her gaze swept over the panorama.

"Ours," he corrected gently. Then he pointed. "See the little farm road that spears across the creek within the waterfall? That's our southern boundary."

"I should have known. The horses...the lovely horses in the pasture."

"Yes, one of them is New Diamond."

She couldn't pick out the yearling from this distance. Her gaze moved on, to a training track, a silo, a long building that reminded her of the barns and stalls at American racetracks.

A wave of emotion swept through her. She had been temporarily distracted by the glamour of the honeymoon and the sight-seeing. Now, in a rush, she felt a return to reality, her reality. How homesick she was for the feel of a horse under her! She felt a sudden, almost painful yearning to go down to the barns, the stalls, to surround herself with the ambience that had been the core of her being since childhood.

Her gaze swung to the house. It was built of weathered stone, rising solidly, commandingly, in a setting of formal gardens, sweeping lawns, walkways bordered by precise low hedges. Like so many structures here in Europe, it was mellowed by the weight of centuries.

The main entry as well as the towering windows were gothically arched. A round belfry rose from one end of

the dull-red tiled roof, a series of open arches support-
ing the belfry cap. Nikki could imagine a fellow armed
with a harquebus posted as a lookout and the bell peal-
ing its tones over the countryside to announce a new
dawn. This house dated back to feudal times. Once
feudal lords had lived there and the land had been tilled
by their serfs.

She exclaimed, "I'll just bet the front entry door is
heavy timbers, darkened with age, strapped with huge
iron hinges."

"Creaks when it opens." Jacques smiled.

"And the main hall has a great, high cathedral ceiling, floors of pegged oak, walls of dark paneling...a
stairway up to a gallery overlooking the main hall.
There must be portraits of ancestors."

"A pretty fair description except for the ancestral
portraits. No suit of armor standing in a corner, I con-
fess. Actually, Nikki, you'll find a rather simple life-
style at Château Trenchard. Only a few thoroughbreds
as compared to what you have at Elmhurst. They are
my avocation, my hobby, my love. Financially, for me
at least, horses are a losing proposition."

"I'm not surprised. You're not by yourself. In
America, the average race horse earns seven thousand
dollars against an annual outlay of training and keeping costs of ten to twenty-five thousand dollars. At
Elmhurst what we lose in one direction we recover from
another, racing, breeding, studding, training, selling,
buying. But even a thoroughbred who doesn't earn his
keep is still as valuable just because of being a
thoroughbred."

"I know exactly what you mean," Jacques said quietly.

She dispelled the turn the talk had taken, giving a laugh. "Well, are you going to dangle me here the rest of the day? What do I have to do to get out there and saddle one of those beauties?"

Obediently, Jacques started the car. As they cruised beside a fenced pasture, Nikki watched the thoroughbreds playfully race the Audi, paralleling the direction of the car.

"Jacques, you have some of the finest-looking stock in the world!"

She was back in her element almost with a jolt. She'd hardly thought of horses during the gossamer honeymoon days, the nights in Jacques's arms! Now it rushed over her, this awareness of who she was, what she was. She couldn't wait to get astride, to feel the power of thoroughbred sinew and heart beneath her, the rush of wind in her face.

Queens could have their thrones, lacquered society matrons their salons! With these horses to ride, she would be the richest woman in the world.

The words of her father came back to her: *...now you've tasted what it's like to win a race. That horse love you've got in your blood isn't going to go away so easily. You might put it out of your mind for a while with the glamour of getting married and all. But somewhere down the line it's going to crop up and eat at you till you won't be able to stand it.*

With an inner smile she thought, Dad, how well you know your daughter!

A wing of sudden anxiety fluttered in her throat. She would have to adapt to the differences in European tracks. National customs, foods, languages...everything so unlike America. Europe was a small, jam-packed continent, really, for all its aura of maturity and the agelessness of medieval cathedrals and village streets of cobblestones. In America, for example, one could travel all day and still be in Texas. Here, you might pass through customs two or three times and hear the same number of dialects and languages in the same geographical distance.

But she had Jacques to coach her in the details that, innocently overlooked, sometimes caused Americans to come off as brash and unlikeable, such as violating a taboo restricted to a principality or making a remark that is a double entendre to European ears.

And racing was racing, wherever you went! The common denominator, the bond that transcended language or national boundary, was in the red blood of the thoroughbred. In the heart of Budapest they ran at Rakoski and trained at Alag, fifteen miles away. Even though nearly a century had passed since Hungarian racing was among the best in the world, you could still get a run for your money in broodlines that had produced Kincsem. In her scrapbook, Nikki had a copy of stamps issued in Hungary to commemorate the great mare.

In iron-curtain country, if you rode in Moscow, it would be at a track with a portentous front entrance worthy of imperial Athens, and you and the Russian competitor could bridge the gaps via Anilin, winner three years running of the Preis von Europa at Cologne and second by a tick in a Washington, D.C., international at Laurel, Maryland.

In Ireland and England, rather than having to overcome problems of language or customs, the trick would be to keep the older tradition that had fathered racing in America from making you feel like an upstart second cousin!

So? Nikki flicked a shoulder. The bottom line would still be to cross the finish line first, whether the horses ran left-right or right-left as a spectator faced the track. American jockeys came over and did it all the time. Look at Cauthen, for example.

And I'll be as good as the best! Nikki thought grimly. I'll show them a ride or two!

She experienced an unexpected twinge of homesickness for Crestland. I haven't forgotten you, she vowed fiercely. One day she'd win the home of her birth back through her racing, and then she and Jacques could divide their time between her American home and his French château.

The rift in their impetuous marriage began over Nikki's intention to resume her career as a professional jockey in Europe. Jacques had other plans, and they did not include having a wife who was a female jockey. He had been well aware of Nikki's passion for horses and racing when they married, but he felt confident that the new life he would create for her would change her priorities. After all, she was little more than a child and as far as Jacques was concerned, risking her life in a sport meant for men was a childish notion that would fade with the right approach.

When she talked about horse racing, he would deftly change the subject. "When you drive into Paris," he said breezily, "you'll enjoy sampling the charge accounts I've set up for you. You'll want to shop at Boucheron for earrings to go with a gown from Balmain. Of course you'll need a pedicure at Shonho in the rue Daniel Casanova that's just right for the Roger Vivier shoes you'll pick out."

When she tried to pin him down about helping her make the right European contacts to embark on a jockey's career, he distracted her with a skiing trip to the Alps or a week spent on a movie set in Rome where he knew the producer and director intimately.

The tactics worked for a while, but they did nothing to change Nikki's basic obsession with horses. She much preferred spending her time in Jacques' stables than using the credit accounts he'd set up for her in the exclusive Paris shops. He often awoke at dawn to find her side of the bed empty. He'd go to the window overlooking the training track and there she'd be, galloping one of his thoroughbreds on an early morning exercise run.

The issue came to a head with a telegram she got early one morning from Colby Cameron. With eyes sparkling, she ran to show it to Jacques, who was having breakfast on the terrace.

"Belmont! Can you believe it? Elvira has a three-year-old she wants me to ride at Belmont!"

Jacques's frown was troubled. "But Nikki, we can't just drop everything and go dashing off to the States for a horse race—"

"Belmont is not just a *horse race*!" Nikki was fairly jumping up and down in her excitement. "It's the big time. I can't pass up something like this!"

"Nikki, Nikki." Tenderly, Jacques drew her down to his lap. "My dear, sweet wife, we need to be reasonable about this. I want you to give up this dangerous notion once and for all of being a professional jockey."

Nikki stiffened. Her eyes blazed and narrowed. "So it's finally out in the open! Jacques Trenchard, I've been suspecting you've been planning to pull something like this. I've brought up the subject a dozen times and you haven't raised one finger to help me get started with any of the European trainers or tracks. I could have ridden your horse in that race last week much better than the jockey you picked! Well, just give me one good reason why I can't race."

"I'll give you two," he said quietly. "Number one, you're a married lady now, the respected wife of a man with a very proud name known all over Europe. I don't relish the idea of having Madame Jacques Trenchard a lady jockey. The scandal tabloids would have a heyday with that! The other thing is the danger involved. I love you, Nikki. I don't want to be in the stands one day and watch my wife get trampled to death on a racetrack."

"You knew when you married me that I was planning to be a professional jockey."

"Yes, but all that has changed. You're married now. You have a whole new life."

The stubborn gazes of two strong personalities met and clashed. Nikki jumped up from his lap, her eyes blazing. "I'm going to America. I'm going to ride at Belmont."

Jacques rose to his feet, a dark flush spreading over his olive complexion. "No, you will not. You're my wife. You'll do as I say."

"Oh, no, I won't!" Nikki cried, beside herself with anger. "If you expected a meek European wife who obeys her macho husband's every command, you picked the wrong woman. I'm going to Belmont!"

And she did. She cried all the way across the Atlantic, but she arrived at Elmhurst Farms stubborn and determined.

The first thing she did was get on a saddle to test her reflexes. She took a big chestnut gelding on a romp around the training track.

In those six swift furlongs, with the clock in her head timing the run to a fraction of a second, furlong by furlong, the feel of stretched-out power beneath her and the wind in her face, a surge of the old feeling came back, giving her the sensation of being totally, vibrantly alive. "I'm as good as I ever was!" she cried exultantly.

The gelding snorted as she impulsively hugged the horse's neck at the end of the run.

She stayed in the saddle to cool the chestnut and walked the animal slowly toward the stables to be washed and curried by a groom.

Walking from the stables in her old familiar chocolate-brown jodhpurs and threadbare-at-the-elbows lightweight sweatshirt, hair windblown around her face, she felt more her true self than she had in months. "To heck with you, Jacques Trenchard," she muttered with a stubborn toss of her head. But then she had to blink hard to clear the tears from her eyes. Why do you have to be a stuffy, hardheaded European aristocrat? she thought miserably. If it just didn't hurt so darn much....

Why did he have to be so stubborn? The fact that she was equally stubborn did not occur to her. She blamed Jacques entirely for their quarrel.

She got a call from Brad Hall. "I knew you'd come back, Nikki! Things are going to be like they used to be for us, aren't they?"

"Brad," she said patiently, "I'm still very much a married woman who loves her husband."

He sounded crushed. "I heard that you broke up with him. I read in one of the gossip columns that you left him."

"Brad, don't believe everything you read. I still love Jacques. We've had a little quarrel over my horse racing, but we'll work things out after my race at Belmont."

"Well, I'm going to Belmont," Brad exclaimed. "I'll be there rooting for you, Nikki."

"Thanks, Brad. I appreciate that."

"Maybe we could at least have a drink or something at the country club. For old times' sake."

"Sure, Brad. We can do that."

That light promise, forgotten a moment later, was the beginning of the end of Nikki's marriage.

Nikki pinned her hopes on Jacques' relenting. She prayed that he'd get over being so stubborn and fly to the States to see her race.

She saw Brad several times before the race. They played a set of tennis at the country club, had drinks with old friends. It helped keep Nikki's mind off her troubles.

At the same time, she discovered with surprise and dismay that she had suddenly become international media gossip material. *Socialite Jockey Splits With Hubby, Flies to States to Race at Belmont*. She read the gossip columns with stunned amazement. From an unknown, scrawny teenager racing at outlaw tracks in Oklahoma, she had been flung into international notoriety. It was understandable, she realized. For one, she had married one of the richest, most eligible men in Europe. That she was also a lady jockey made her news material. Add the spice of a marriage split and rumors about being seen with another man, and newshounds had the perfect ingredients for a juicy scandal. She saw photos of herself running horses on the exercise track at Elmhurst and other shots of her with Brad at the country club. The idea of a triangle involving Brad Hall was laughable to her. But maybe not to an outsider, and maybe not to Jacques, if he read the stories.

At first she was dismayed, then she decided perhaps it might bring Jacques to his senses. She had fantasies of his rushing to the States to fight for his bride.

Brad drove over to Elmhurst late one afternoon. She had been out, riding hard for an hour on the exercise track. She was walking from the stables when Brad's car drove up. He waved and approached her. "It's buffet night at the country club. Want to go have dinner with me?"

"All right. I'm hungry enough to eat a horse."

"Not one of Elvira's thoroughbreds, I hope."

"Hardly." She laughed. "You have to give me time to take a shower and change."

"No hurry."

He trailed upstairs after her. It was a perfectly natural thing for him to do. Brad had been an informal member of the Elmhurst family for years. His family owned a neighboring breeding farm. He took it for granted there was always an extra plate at the time if he happened to wander over at mealtime.

Colby Cameron tolerated the young man because he was close friends with Brad's father, but he often got mad over the trouble Nikki and Brad got into together. "I'd run him off," he once told Nikki after one of their scrapes, "except I can't really blame him. He's probably no worse influence on you than you are on him!"

That was back in Nikki's wilder, rebellious teenage years. She had simply given her father a defiant look and stalked off. As she grew up and tamed down to some degree, their escapades tapered off, but Brad continued to hang around, considering Elmhurst his second home.

Now, she thought nothing of it when Brad trailed after her into her room and sprawled on the bed to read a magazine while she went into her bathroom to take a shower. Her mind was filled with the race she would ride in a few days and with Jacques. Her feelings about him ranged from waves of fury to moments of heartache. She missed him terribly, longed to feel the safe comfort of his arms around her. If they could only work out their differences! Many women these days combined marriage with a career. If she'd just stick to her guns, she told herself, Jacques would eventually give in. That is, he would if he really loved her....

If he really loved her. That was the question that nagged and hurt the most. They had known each other such a short time, had married so impetuously. Suppose it had only been an infatuation to Jacques? Maybe he'd been intrigued by her because she was different from the European social jet-set women he'd been running around with, and when the first glamour of the honeymoon wore off, he'd discovered he wasn't actually in love at all. She'd spent many sleepless nights wrestling with that dismal thought.

Now she tried to put the thoughts out of her mind as she stood under the stinging shower spray. She couldn't allow herself to brood. She had to keep her mind on the race or she'd do a miserable job. It was good that Brad was around to cheer her up and take her over to the country club. They'd see old friends, laugh, have a good time, get her mind off her problems....

She stepped out of the shower, dried and slipped on a robe. Her hair curled around her face in damp tendrils. She'd do something with it after she picked out a dress for tonight.

Barefooted, she padded from the bathroom back into the bedroom.

What happened next was like something out of a ridiculous silent movie melodrama, a scene Nikki would replay endlessly in the years that followed. Brad was comfortably situated on the bed, propped against pillows, shoes off, legs crossed. Nikki was on her way to the closet. The bedroom door was partly ajar. Then it was pushed open. Jacques Trenchard stood framed in the doorway.

For a moment, the tableau was frozen. Nikki stood there, her eyes widening. Jacques' black-eyed gaze swung from Brad sprawled on the bed to Nikki. It was obvious from the way the robe clung to her body, still damp from the shower, that she had nothing on under it. The blood drained from Jacques' face.

Nikki's first reaction was complete surprise, followed by joy at seeing Jacques there. She started toward him with a happy cry rising to her lips. But the cold fury in his eyes stopped her like a fist slammed into her face.

In bitter tones, through stiff lips, Jacques said, "I didn't believe the gossip columns. Now I see it's true."

"Jacques," Nikki said with a flash of anger, "don't be an idiot!"

"Oh, I've been the fool all right," Jacques said coldly. "I can see I'm an intruder. You belong here with your horses and your lover. It was a mistake for me to come here into your life in the first place."

Brad uncoiled from the bed. "Hey, look, fellah—"

But Jacques silenced him with a look of pure murder. "I suppose I should kill you. But she isn't worth it. Go ahead and enjoy her. You obviously had her long before I came along."

"How dare you stand there and make accusations without letting me explain!" Nikki cried furiously.

He turned and stalked out.

A week later Nikki was notified by Jacques' attorneys that legal proceedings were under way to have their marriage annulled.

It was several weeks later that Colby, hearing Nikki's muffled sobs, came up to her room to comfort her. He held her in his arms, clumsily stroking her hair. "Honey, I know there isn't much I can say that will make it any easier. Things like this take time. You'll get over the hurt after a while. The guy just isn't worth tearing yourself to pieces over—''

Nikki shook her head miserably. "Dad, it's worse than that. I'm pregnant."

For a moment, surprise kept Colby silent. "How long have you known, honey?"

"I just found out."

"Hmmm." Her father scratched his jaw thoughtfully. "I don't mean to interfere, but don't you think this will change everything? I mean, when Jacques finds out he's going to be a father he might have second thoughts about this annulment business—''

Nikki's tear-reddened eyes looked at her father, then away. "I can't tell him."

"But why not?" Colby gasped. "I know you're mad at him, but he's got a right to know he's going to have a child—''

"Don't you see, Dad?" Nikki sighed. "He's convinced I was having an affair with Brad. He's got it in his head that Brad and I were lovers before I met him and we took up where we left off when I came back to the States. Now if I tell him I'm pregnant, he'd only say it was Brad's child."

She shook her head, raising her chin with an air of her old stubborn defiance. "To hell with Jacques Trenchard. I don't need him and my child doesn't need him. We'll make out just fine by ourselves."

Nikki went into seclusion, hiding from nosy gossip mongers and reporters. Somehow it was important to her that Jacques not find out she was pregnant. She was certain he would believe the child was Brad's and it would confirm his jealous suspicions. She had her son at a cousin's home in Tennessee and succeeded in keeping the fact from the newspapers and from Jacques.

Johnny was six months old before Nikki resumed her riding career.

From an inconsequential line on a track program, her name began appearing in sports page subheads; then, as she rode winners in more and more important races, her name and picture appeared prominently in print and in feature stories. Finally she had a guest spot on a TV interview show and the story of her career was written about in a slick women's magazine. The trophy case at Elmhurst was enlarged as she steadily added silver.

Six years had passed since Jacques had had their marriage annulled. The chapter of her life involving Jacques Trenchard was a heartbreak she endeavored to put behind her. Her life revolved around her son and her career. The ultimate goal of her efforts was always shining and clear before her. She lived now for the day when her growing bank account would put her in a position to reclaim Crestland. What a proud day that would be! She had promised not only herself, but her son as well, that one day they would walk proudly into the halls of that stately mansion, coming home to the land that should have been her birthright.

The money she could have made riding Spanish Lady across the finish line a winner at Gulfstream would have put her a large step closer to her goal. That triumph had been wrenched from her grasp by a vicious little jockey with the face of a cherub. And now her leg was in a cast and the only remaining chance of a windfall big enough to buy Crestland would be to win the Derby itself.

But suddenly, with her father's stunning news everything came crashing down around her. Jacques Trenchard had suddenly come back into her life. He was the owner of Crestland.

Chapter Eight

Stunned by the news her father had given her, Nikki rose and hobbled to the window of her father's office. From there she could see the vast pastureland of Elmhurst. Beyond it, hidden by the rolling meadows and wooded creeks, was Crestland.

She felt an unreasoning wave of resentment. "What right did he have to come back here and buy Crestland?"

Her father smiled wryly. "I suppose the right any man has with enough of a bankroll. And whatever other shortcomings Jacques Trenchard might have, being short of money isn't one of them."

"Yes, but why?" She directed the question to herself as much as to her father. A cloud of worry darkened her hazel eyes. "D'you suppose it has anything to do with Johnny?"

"That thought has entered my mind," her father admitted with a nod.

A sudden, uneasy chill caused Nikki to shudder. "But why, after all these years..."

"You kept Johnny pretty well under wraps those first years," Colby reminded her. "It's just been recently, since you've gotten so much publicity, that the news media has found out you're a mother as well as a jockey. Maybe he didn't know about Johnny before."

A frown stenciled her brow as she shook her head. "It seems terribly farfetched. Still, I can't think of any other reason why he'd move in next door...."

Colby shrugged. "Well, it could be a coincidence. He's a horse lover. Maybe word got around international circles that Crestland was up for sale. Maybe he couldn't pass up the opportunity to own such a fine piece of Kentucky real estate."

"He had no right!" Nikki fumed, slamming her right fist into her left palm. Tears suddenly blurred her vision. She choked, "That's my home. I've planned for years to buy it back. I'd have the money, too, if we win the Derby."

Colby rose from his desk and gently put his arm around her. "Honey, that's an awfully big 'if.' I know how much that place means to you. But if it just doesn't work out, you know you've always got a home here. As far as Elvira is concerned, you're a daughter to her."

"I know, Dad." She sighed. "But it's not the same."

There was no point in talking about it. She knew that Colby had never understood her obsession to live at

Crestland again. Land was important to him only as a place to graze his beloved thoroughbreds.

Nikki was on edge as the days passed. The thought that Jacques Trenchard had become her next-door neighbor kept her in a constant state of emotional turmoil.

Her gloomy state of mind was somewhat brightened when the cast was removed from her leg. She limped a bit, favoring the still tender limb, but she was grateful that she could begin riding. "Take it easy at first, young lady," the doctor had warned. "No galloping around the exercise track at full speed for a while."

The first time Nikki grasped the reins, she felt her palms grow damp. Perched in the saddle, she was aware of a queasiness in her stomach. There was a flash of painful memory, the terrifying sensation of hurtling through the air, the sickening shock of the earth's impact.

She swore under her breath, fighting away the memories. Was it going to be like this every time she got on a horse? What's the matter with you? she chastised herself furiously. This isn't the first time you've been hurt falling from a horse.

But this time it was different, a ghostly voice warned her. This time it reached deeper inside her and wouldn't let go.

Furiously, she wrenched the horse away from the groom and rode out on the exercise track. This was just something else she had to lick, the way she'd licked the other bad things in her life: the death of her grandfather and mother, the loss of her home, the discrimination against women jockeys, the breakup of her marriage....

She walked the horse, every movement reminding her of the damage that had been done to her physical resources. One time around the track and she felt sore and tired. Obviously it was going to take some hard training and conditioning to get back in shape.

As she rode slowly back from the track, her attention was suddenly drawn to another rider coming up the path from the outer gate.

She reined back and sat watching, her heart picking up tempo. She knew even from this distance who the rider was. She'd seen him too often on a polo field. No other man could ride a horse with such grace and ease.

It was Jacques Trenchard.

She sat immobilized as he drew nearer. Emotions churned wildly through her being—all the feelings she had lived with for the past six years. Anger and bitterness struggled furiously with bittersweet regret. How could she hate him so for the way he'd treated her and still feel this ball of excitement spinning inside her?

Damn, he looks good on a horse, she thought helplessly. She despised him and at the same time she thought it wasn't fair that he should look so elegant, so masculine, so commanding on a horse. All the legends of heroes on gallant steeds raced through her thoughts—a fiery cossack leading a cavalry charge... King Arthur...El Cid. What was it about being astride a horse that emphasized a man's masculinity?

He wore shiny leather riding boots and trousers. His white turtleneck sweater accented his olive complexion, the flashing blackness of his eyes and the midnight darkness of his thick, wavy hair. He grasped the reins in strong, tanned fingers.

Those searing black eyes burned to the very core of her being as he pulled his horse to a stop beside her. For a moment, neither of them spoke. Then he said, "I'm glad to see you have recovered, Nikki. That was a nasty spill you took at Gulfstream."

"What difference does it make to you?" she asked coldly.

He gazed at her steadily, confusing her with emotions in his dark eyes that she couldn't interpret. "I was concerned," he said quietly. "I checked with the hospital in Florida to make sure you were going to be all right. Did you receive my flowers?"

She nodded briefly, not trusting her voice.

"I didn't ask to visit you then because I was afraid it would upset you."

Boy, that's the understatement of the year! she thought grimly.

"I've been waiting until I knew you had fully recovered to visit you. Nikki, I have to talk to you."

All the bitterness of his unjust rejection six years before welled up to her lips. "I have nothing to talk to you about," she said.

"I'm sorry, but I think we do."

She had forgotten how the resonant timbre of his voice could demoralize her. He still had the slight French accent that added its special elegant charm. She tried desperately not to look at the outlines of his chest and broad shoulders so clearly defined by the tight sweater.

"I'm busy," she said shortly. "If it's about horses or business, you'll have to see my father."

She started to pull away, but he reached out and caught her reins. "It's about business, yes, but personal business. It's you I have to talk to."

"I can't image what we'd possibly have to talk about."

"Can't you?"

She tried but couldn't escape the intensity of his gaze.

His horse pawed the ground impatiently, tossed his head and tried to move away. Jacques reined him back. He said, "This is hardly the place to hold a serious conversation, on two restless horses. Will you have dinner with me tonight, Nikki, so we can talk?"

She drew a breath, trying to rein in her tumultuous emotions the way he had pulled back his horse. "I don't want to have dinner with you, Jacques. I told you I have nothing to talk with you about."

She started to pull her horse away from him, but his hand moved to catch her reins. His intense gaze paralyzed her. He said, "I've come to talk to you about your son, Johnny."

Her mouth went dry. "What—what business is my son to you?"

"Quite a bit, I think," he murmured. "He's my son, too, isn't he, Nikki?"

Chapter Nine

That night, seated at a table across from Jacques, Nikki clasped her cold hands and tried to hold on to some semblance of orderly thought. She must have been out of her mind to agree to this meeting, she thought.

He had taken her to a rustic, beautifully preserved Kentucky tavern, an historic site, that had been a food and lodging way stop for travelers in colonial times. Stephen Foster had once been a guest in this fine old house and had immortalized it in his song, "My Old Kentucky Home." Notices on the wall from that bygone era read "Gentlemen lodgers will sleep in north end of loft; ladies in south section. Traffic between north and south area of loft is forbidden. Gentlemen carrying valuables are advised to retire with pistol under pillow."

But Nikki was oblivious to the picturesque, historical surroundings. "Jacques, please stay out of my life," she said, tears starting to burn her eyes. "And out of Johnny's. You've caused me enough trouble."

She tried unsuccessfully to interpret the cloud of emotions that swirled through his eyes. For a moment he seemed lost and unsure of what to say next. She wondered if she had touched a vulnerable spot, but she saw that his jaw remained stubbornly set. "I can understand your bitterness," he said, his words slow and firm. "Nevertheless, I would like to see my son."

She raised her chin, her eyes bright with anger. "What has you so interested in your son after six years?"

His dark eyes blazed with anger. "For six years I didn't know I had a son!" he exclaimed. "Nikki, you had no right to keep the boy a secret from me."

"Oh, look who's suddenly so self-righteous!" she flung back at him. "I wasn't the one who went storming back to France and had the marriage annulled."

"That was a problem that concerned you and me, not my son. You seem to be of the opinion that only a mother cares about her children. For your information, a father's instinct and love for his child can be just as strong."

For a moment his impassioned words caught her off guard. But then the old anger rekindled. She was too human to pass up the opportunity of reminding him of his unjust accusations six years ago. "What makes you so sure Johnny is your son? I think the last thing you said to me was that I was having an affair with Brad

Hall. How do you know Johnny's father isn't Brad Hall?''

She flung the words at him with all the pent-up hurt and bitterness of the past six years, her voice breaking.

He brought his gaze back to her face, brooding now, his eyes dark and thoughtful. "A lot of things were said in anger. Perhaps I accused you unjustly. But I had no idea you were going to have a child."

"How did you suddenly find out about Johnny?"

"A few months ago, someone called my attention to some article about you in a women's magazine. There were a number of pictures. You on a horse after a race. You at home. You with your son, Johnny. It gave me quite a jolt. When I saw the boy's photograph, I saw myself as a boy, looking out of that magazine page." He nodded soberly. "Yes, he's my son, Nikki."

She swallowed with difficulty, then shrugged. "That's neither here nor there. You gave up all rights to Johnny when you walked out of my life and had the marriage annulled. I had Johnny by myself. I've raised him by myself. You have no right to come barging back into our lives at this point."

"But I tell you, I didn't know you were pregnant—"

"It wouldn't have mattered!" she cried. "You walked out on me because you didn't want a jockey for a wife."

Their verbal exchange reached an impasse. There was a deadly silence that stretched for several moments.

Finally Jacques asked, "What have you told the boy about his father?"

"I told him that his father was dead. As far as I was concerned, he was—and is."

Again the strange look in Jacques' eyes that she was unable to interpret. Was it pain? Was it regret? Or was there something else mingled—a threat of some kind.

With a sudden feeling of fright, she said, "You have no legal claim on Johnny whatsoever, if that's what you're thinking."

"Nobody is talking about legalities," he said with a frown.

"Then why did you suddenly buy Crestland—move in next door? You're up to something, Jacques Trenchard, and I want to know what it is!"

He sighed. "I told you. I saw the magazine story and realized I had a son I've never seen, never held, never spoken to. At the same time, a real estate broker told me the Crestland property was on the market at a fair price. There's nothing sinister about my actions. I just want to see my son, to let him know his father isn't dead, that he's very much alive and would like to get to know him. Buying the property next door seemed like an opportune thing to do under the circumstances."

Nikki looked down at her hands fumbling nervously with a napkin.

Jacques went on, "Nikki, this is just a personal matter between us. I'm not here with any kind of legal threat. Don't you think Johnny has a right to know his father? Is it fair to him to do that?"

"I—I don't know. I haven't been prepared for anything like this. I have to give it a lot of thought. It would be a big shock to Johnny. How could I break this kind of news to him? How could I explain that I lied about his father being dead? What would it do to him?"

"I should think it would make him very happy."

That statement was a powerful blow. She had no answer to it. As much as she hated to admit it, she knew how much Johnny longed to have a real father, how he talked about other boys, his friends, and their fathers.

"I—I just don't know," she repeated. "I have to think about."

The meal came. She bent over her plate but only toyed with her food. She felt Jacques' eyes on her. His gaze gave her a tense, prickly sensation.

She tried to stifle hurting memories that tugged at her heart, but they were stronger than her will. Being this close to Jacques brought it all back vividly, their first kiss that had shaken her to the depths of her being, his touch that could make her feel alive all over, the sweet, quiet moments they had shared. She remembered his tenderness, the sound of his voice at night, his head on the pillow beside hers. She remembered holding his hand on a Paris street in the rain and suddenly turning into a doorway with him for a laughing, carefree kiss.

How could such beautiful, shimmering romantic love end so tragically? She had been so young, hardly more than a teenager. Perhaps if she had been older, more experienced, she could have handled their problems with more wisdom.

There had been that basic difference in their backgrounds. His traditional European upbringing had him convinced that, as his wife, Nikki should obey his wishes in the matter of her career. That point of view had run headlong into her American spirit of independence, which had insisted that he should compromise and be reasonable about interests that were a vital part of her life, her spirit, her self-identity. But he wouldn't compromise. Neither would she. The result had been a clash between two equally strong, stubborn personalities.

And there had been his jealousy of Brad. Could she blame him for that? she had sometimes wondered. She had to admit he'd had plenty of grounds for his suspicions. Guiltily, she remembered how she had once taunted Jacques with Brad when she was first fighting her attraction for him. Then, when Jacques had found Nikki and Brad in her bedroom—how compromising that must have looked.

What was the use of going over the past? She had done that a thousand times in the last six years, as if somehow thinking about it could repair it—like a tearful child holding a broken doll in its hand, wanting it to be back together the way it once had been. But childish wishing didn't make it so.

Now she stole a glance at Jacques, her breath catching in her throat at the sight of his handsome face. She was unprepared for the wave of desire that his nearness awakened in her. The memory of abandoned lovemaking in his arms became a burning warmth spreading through her body, making her aware of the dress fabric touching her thighs. She felt as if her breasts were swollen. How could she hate him and still feel this arousal of passion? It was as if her body, longing for his, knew only the fundamental chemistry that still existed between them, ignoring the logic of her mind.

She felt her cheeks grow warm with embarrassment at the fantasies that burned through her mind. A primitive urge she couldn't control made her yearn to reach out, to touch his cheek, then open the buttons of his shirt and plow through the mat of hair on his chest to stroke him and know him intimately once again. Her gaze trailed to the contours of his lips. She felt a hunger in her mouth for his. With a desperate effort, she snatched her gaze away from him.

Then she wondered, what was he thinking now? Was he, too, remembering what they had once shared? Or had it not been that important to him? Had he ever really loved her? Sometimes she wondered if she'd meant anything to him at all. Perhaps he'd never given her a second thought after the marriage ended.

During the past six years, she had caught glimpses of him in newspapers and tabloids. With his far-flung interests in European horse racing, shipping and real estate development scattered from the North Sea to the Mediterranean, he remained one of the continent's most eligible bachelors, always material for a gossip column. He was seen regularly at Monte Carlo, at the Cannes Film Festival or a grand prix race, usually accompanied by a beautiful woman. Why had he never remarried? she sometimes wondered. His latest romantic interest was the beautiful actress Gina Anotia, the woman Nikki had seen with him at Gulfstream the fateful day of her accident.

She suddenly realized his brooding gaze had settled on her again. He was looking at her as if stripping away her garments to uncover the lovely secrets that had once been his. His eyes ranged over her hair, her face, her throat, her bosom, causing her flesh to grow warm and tingly wherever his gaze touched.

As it if were not possible to be near her without physically touching her, he suddenly reached across the table and captured her hand. She felt disconcerted, confused. She tried to pull her hand away, but he held it firmly, making her feel weak. She wanted to look away but his gaze was hypnotic. She felt as if she were drowning in the black depths of his eyes.

He said quietly, "You're as lovely as ever, Nikki. Even more desirable than I remembered. You have blossomed in the past six years."

Nikki stood at her bedroom window, looking down at the man on horseback and the boy beside him on the pony. The boy was looking up at the man, his face radiant, his eyes bright with excitement. The man was gazing down at the boy with an expression of love and happiness.

Nikki felt her heart fill until she had to strain to catch her breath. A film of tears blurred the scene below.

For a solid week she had waged an inner battle that had almost pushed her over the brink. Finally, she had accepted what her heart told her was the right decision. No matter how she might feel about Jacques, it wasn't fair to Johnny to keep him from knowing his father.

It had taken the last ounce of her nerve to break the news to Johnny. She had rehearsed her speech for an entire sleepless night. The next morning she rode out to their special place on the hill overlooking Crestland. Johnny was in the saddle in front of her. She swung down and reached up to help her son to the ground.

"Got something special to tell you," she began, trying to hide her nervousness from him.

Johnny looked at her quizzically, then at the view of Crestland in the distance. His eyes brightened with excitement. "We're gonna move back to our real home?"

She smoothed his hair fondly. "Nope. Maybe someday. That isn't the big news." She drew a deep breath and swallowed. God, help me to say the right words, she silently prayed. "Y'know, you sometimes talk about having a real dad. That would be kind of neat, wouldn't it?"

"Sure," he exclaimed. Then his eyes became sober. "But my father is up in heaven. You told me—"

Nikki touched her tongue to her dry lips. "What if I told you I'd made a mistake about that...if I'd found out he's really still alive?"

Johnny frowned, looking puzzled. "You mean the man in the picture you showed me?"

"Yes."

He still looked baffled, struggling to put this into a five-year-old's comprehension of things. Finally he asked, "Did God let him out of heaven?"

Nikki felt the tension in her explode in laughter. "Not exactly like that, sweetheart," she said. She thought to herself, I'm not all that sure they'd allow that scoundrel into heaven in the first place! To Johnny, she said, "It's all pretty complicated to explain, honey. Y'see, this man, your father, Jacques Trenchard, and I were married. Then he went back to France before you were born. I—I didn't exactly lie to you when I told you he was dead. Grown-ups sometimes feel like someone has died when they put that person out of their lives. That's grown-up stuff, hard for a five-year-old to understand.

Anyway, I didn't think we'd ever see him again, so he was as good as dead to us, wasn't he?"

"Did—did he know about me?"

"No, he didn't. And I didn't think he'd care about you if he did know. Well, guess what; I was very wrong about that. He recently found out about you and he came storming over here from his home across the sea and he wants to see you in the worst way."

Johnny's eyes had grown as large as saucers. "My real Dad? Gee."

Nikki remained silent while the news sank in. She watched the growing excitement in Johnny's eyes. "Where—where is he now?"

"Well, that's the best part. See our real home down there?" She pointed at Crestland. "He just bought it and he's living there, right next door to us."

"Golly," the boy said with a note of awe.

"Yeah; golly," she admitted. "That's pretty earth-shaking news, huh?"

Johnny nodded, his eyes as bright as a pair of dark marbles.

"Want to see him?"

Again the boy nodded, suddenly looking shy and uncertain. "I—I guess so."

"I know all of this takes a little getting used to. You'll have to get acquainted with him, but I think you'll like him. He likes horses. He has a bunch. He wants to ride over with a pony he's picked out for you, if that's okay."

The excitement came back. "Yeah, gee!"

"Tomorrow. He wants to come tomorrow. Is that okay?"

Johnny gulped and nodded.

For the rest of the day he pestered her constantly, wanting to know how much longer until tomorrow. That night it took him two hours to go to sleep. Emotionally drained and exhausted, Nikki went to her room and flopped on her bed. Staring up at the ceiling, she thought about the look of anticipation and wonder on her son's face. A real, sure-enough Dad. Golly. She smiled weakly. Thank you, God, she thought. I think I did the right thing.

Then she thought: It sure isn't easy, being a parent. Especially a single parent!

In the days that followed, she was aware of a creeping, newly formed habit. She would awaken in the morning and find herself slipping to her window for a look in the direction of Crestland. She would think of Jacques rising over there. And that would trigger a memory of a bed with his warmth lingering, of the way the muscles in his chest would ridge when he took his first morning stretch, of the first lazing of his waking eyes, the way his sleep-tousled hair would drop a lock across his high forehead, like a question mark that asked: Shall we really get up or just spend the morning in bed?

She would twist from the window with the defensive movement of a kitten about to snarl. She tried to fill her mind with other things, start her day determinedly. She would refuse to think about him living over there, so close. She would not—repeat, not—catch herself taking a quick breath as a strange car came up the driveway or a non-Elmhurst horse and rider crested a hill or the voice of a visitor filtered from the hallway.

It was inevitable that once he had broken the ice, he would become a regular visitor to Elmhurst to see his son. He maintained a polite, formal role when he was in Nikki's presence. She managed to be alone with him as infrequently as possible. But even when there were others present, he had the ability to make her feel as if no one else was in the room except the two of them. He could look at others, nod, chat, but by some mysterious process his eyes were for her alone. And she was acutely aware of their searching, the lurking, primitive power in their depths, their questing, seeking. Was he reliving the intimate moments of their honeymoon in France...or was she imagining it? Once, walking out of a room, feeling his gaze, she glanced over her shoulder. She'd gotten a giddying glimpse of herself walking away and his eyes following her movements, remembering that heart-shaped little birthmark just above the swell of her right hip.

"Let me make friends with Johnny," he'd said. She had agreed and she watched the quick development of a friendship. Two peas out of the same genetic pod, they even sat a saddle with the same natural ease, the erectness of shoulders, the tilt of face. The sunlight caught the same highlights in two heads of windblown hair.

Daisybud was the pony Jacques had given Johnny. The relationship between the boy and the animal was that of boy to puppy. If Johnny appeared, Daisybud would race across a pasture to nuzzle him, receive his scratch and caress, flicking her ears, swishing her lustrous tail and mane, communicating. She would wait impatiently for Johnny to mount, snapping her head around as if saying, "Hey, fellow, get aboard or I'll bite your backside."

That first day Jacques had brought the pony and he and Johnny had jogged off together, Nikki had stood at her bedroom window, watching, unable to move her eyes until they'd dipped out of sight beyond a low rise. She'd turned away then, almost overcome with emotion. Her heart had ached with the thought of how things might have turned out if they could have been a family.

Chapter Ten

Two questions had lurked at the edge of Nikki's mind after the spill at Gulfstream. Would her leg be okay? How would she react in a crucial moment on a fast track?

She could answer the first. Basically, she was as healthy as little Johnny's frisky pony. Out of shape, perhaps, and the leg was weak from nonuse, but her physical stamina and the right conditioning would bring her back to normal quickly.

The second question was more troubling. Most jockeys shared the fatalistic attitude of auto racers and test pilots. You trained and prepared to the nth degree so the odds were in your favor. Then you got on with the job. Fine so far. But doing the job after impersonal hazard had become a very personal reality, a psychologically scarring experience, wasn't the same piece of cake. In most hazardous occupations the process was known as separating the men from the boys, a chauvinistic phraseology that made Nikki laugh while at the same time agreeing with the basic idea.

Only an idiot ignored the reality of the hazards, and when a severe injury occurred anywhere on a racetrack, jockeys idling in rec rooms a thousand miles away felt a unique impact at the news. While they unracked a cue stick or squinted at a dartboard's bull's-eye or bumped a fifty-cent game on the strength of three aces, the question hovered: What if it had happened to me? How would I come back?

Most came back in good style. A few lost it, that added drop of starch that takes apparently reckless advantage of a slot between two leaders, a slight drift from the rail on the far turn by the horse ahead. These overly cautious riders could be successfully challenged, nerve pitted against nerve. A small minority tried for a while and eventually left their saddles in the tackroom, letting someone else wear the silks.

Despite repeated assurances to herself, despite her outward jauntiness, Nikki had a new sense of awareness of the skittish thoroughbred beneath her the day she started seriously retraining. A sense of her frailty on controlling this half ton of raw, headstrong animal power almost overwhelmed her. Her mind flashed to that moment at Gulfstream when it had seemed certain that she and Spanish Lady were out of control, tumbling in a ghastly pinwheel of helpless limbs in the path of tons of stampeding horseflesh.

This morning she slipped quietly to the training track, permitting only Orlis to saddle the stallion and come with her.

He stood at the horse's withers, holding the rein close to the D bit, which was preferred at most racetracks. He looked up. She was perched in the saddle, wearing Elmhurst silks, highly polished boots, riding pants, Caliente helmet. She didn't know why, but she'd gotten up this morning with the overpowering compulsion to ride this first day dressed as for the kill in a stakes race, looking like a winner. Perhaps it had been a gesture to bolster her morale. If Orlis had expected her to appear in workaday garb—boots, jeans, old sweat shirt—he'd made no comment.

Now he spoke, almost for the first time since their perfunctory greeting in the barns.

"Sweating?"

She nodded.

The mellow deep brown eyes in the aging face regarded her. "Me, too," he said, "and I've got no real reason at all, have I?"

"You trying to tell me something?"

"Me? Tell you? Who knows thoroughbreds better than Nikki Cameron, who can practically talk to them? And who could ever tell Nikki Cameron anything?"

She felt the twitchings through the saddle. The stallion wanted to rear. Her stomach was in knots. Her palms were slippery holding the reins. Would she ever overcome this dark cloud, this threat of sickening fear when she was mounted and her mind was trying to fill the empty track ahead with imaginary horses wildly careening, veering, rearing as they tried to avoid her prone body in their mad forty-miles-an-hour rush? ...

She heard Orlis speak from a distance.

"Don't fight it. Don't try to deny it." His voice was flat, unsympathetic, like a force turning her face to view a specter head-on.

"Easy for you to say," she snapped through brittle lips.

"Well, what's the choice? A trainer can train and a jockey can ride, and in the end it all boils down to who's the thoroughbred."

She felt alone, isolated. She wanted to grind her teeth and cry at the same time.

"Orlis, you are the cruelest, meanest old man in the state of Kentucky!"

"Hot damn! Got the old vinegar bubbling! Now, you let him run a little, but don't overdo the first day."

"I happen to know a little something about riding a horse," she said acidly.

"Then do it," he said placidly.

In the days that followed, she trained hard, to the limits of pent-up energies and endurance, exercising with weights and cycle to strengthen her leg. She did calisthenics with little Johnny beside her, filling her heart in his aping of her movements. "Wow!" Toweling her face, she would reach to grip little-boy biceps. "I sure wouldn't want to be the schoolyard bully who misreads a certain fellow's good manners and politeness."

He grinned. "My dad says I'll make a great ball player. He's going to teach me how to throw a curve ball."

Nikki swallowed hard to get the lump out of her throat. Jacques had certainly won the boy over in a short while. Johnny idolized him. She had mixed feelings about that. She resented Jacques' sudden intrusion in her life, and in the closeness that Johnny had only shared with her. At the same time, she recognized the need of a boy to have a male adult figure in his life as a role model. It would be difficult to find a more masculine role model than Jacques Trenchard!

Colby Cameron brought Nikki's horse, Banshee, in for a few days' rest after a meet at nearby Keeneland. The big black stallion with white stocking legs and star on his forehead whickered a greeting when Nikki ran out to the barn to welcome him home. He thrust his head over the gate rail to receive the covert sugar cube from her hand.

"Too much of that," Colby complained, "and he'll have a jawful of cavities."

As Nikki strolled back to the house with her father, she knew they were sharing a thought, a question. In his last three races Banshee had won once, showed another time and then had eaten dirt as a dismal also-ran. Against this were the times and performances of stakes winners scattered from New York to California. The Derby this year was going to draw one of the strongest fields ever. Banshee was beginning to look like a long shot in the event that his nomination was accepted.

"The wrong jockey has been riding him," Nikki said at last, entering the house as her father held the kitchen door open for her. "Dad, we simply can't blow it during the qualifying races. So I'm going to do some warm-

ups in minor events starting this weekend at Charles
Town. Then I'm going aboard Banshee.''

"You sure you're up to it?'' he asked, looking at her
closely.

"Yes.''

"In every way?''

She knew the question he was really asking. How
were the reflexes and reactions of a jockey who came
close to being killed at Gulfstream?

"In every way,'' she replied with a firmness she
wished she could thoroughly feel.

"We'll see.'' Colby patted her shoulder. "Meantime, I guess I should shower and get ready for Elvira's
dinner.''

Elvira's dinner. Nikki faced the event with a mixture
of dread and tension. The event hadn't been far from
Nikki's mind all day, busy as she had been. Every so
often, Elvira liked to throw a big dinner and invited all
the important owners of horse farms in the area as well
as a sprinkling of state politicians and other VIPs. The
guest list often read like a *Who's Who* of Kentucky
horse breeding. The dinners were formal, Irish linen on
the table, Tiffany silver highly polished, the rarest wine
from the Elmhurst cellar, a chef and maître d' brought
over from Lexington to assist the Elmhurst chef.

Elvira would not have dreamed of excluding Jacques
Trenchard, her next-door neighbor. It would have been
an affront that would have had all of Kentucky talk-
ing. After all, she'd had business dealings with Jacques
Trenchard long before Nikki met him in the first place.
He was internationally known in horse racing society.
Elvira was well aware of the awkward situation involv-

ing Nikki, but she had explained that she was obligated to invite Jacques. Maybe he won't come, Nikki hoped. But his R.S.V.P. was in the affirmative.

Nikki considered pleading a headache and staying in her room. But she decided that would be cowardly. She had as much right at the table as he did. Why should she run off and hide?

From the cook's grumbling, Nikki knew that tonight's menu included escargot. Her mind flashed to the dinner in Paris when Jacques had introduced her to the French delicacy. She couldn't stop herself from recalling what had followed, when she and Jacques...the Lotti hotel suite bed...Well, he'd warned her in advance that the beds at the Lotti were excellently large....

She had a basic black satin Givenchy that should do nicely. It was a cocktail dress designed with a simplicity that was always in style. The length, just below the knee, revealed a glimpse of her calves. The bodice dared a hint of the swell of her creamy breasts. Rhinestones clipped the startlingly black lines on either shoulder, leaving her slender neck entirely exposed. It was the sort of dress she could wear to stunning effect, formal yet careless of formality, staid yet slyly provocative. She laughed when she thought how out of character it was for her. What a contrast to her usual attire of casual jeans and baseball cap or boots and riding silks! But tonight she had a strong urge to look utterly feminine. Why? She dodged the question.

As she laid the gown out, Jacques crept inexorably into her thoughts. She could almost feel the warmth of his breath against her ear, the nibbling of his lips, his passion-thickened whisper. "You can wear anything and make it look Dior, even coveralls in a yearling barn, but I prefer you this way...as we are, away from all the world.... I like you in nothing at all...."

Her jaws tightened against the memory and yet it teased at her lasciviously. It stirred a primitive hunger, a heat deep within her. It made her swear at Jacques Trenchard and the memories that wouldn't leave her alone. In the bathroom she stripped for the shower and turned the water on icy cold. She needed that stinging spray.

Skies were darkening prematurely from massive, sullen clouds. Gusts of wind were beginning to whip the tall elms along the long driveway when the first guests arrived—the Tomkinses, a robust, middle-aged couple. K. R. was an ex–lieutenant governor of the state. He glanced up at the thickening clouds.

"Well, nothing could be warmer or friendlier than Elvira Ledbetter's house on a wild, stormy night! How are you, Elvira? And Nikki. My dear, you are positively ravishing! Nothing like a good athletic life in Kentucky to keep that figure the envy of the world."

As the house filled with arriving guests, the first flicker of lightning split the sky. A dash of rain lashed the windows. Nikki couldn't escape the feeling that something in the stormy night matched her own inner turbulence.

He was coming.

He wasn't coming.

She moved about, chatting with people she'd long known, people with whom she was comfortable. It could have been such a pleasant evening....

Why didn't he show? Or phone and give an excuse to Elvira?

Then, as they were having predinner cocktails, he was suddenly standing in the entry hall, rain spotting his trench coat and clinging to his windblown hair like sparkling diamonds.

His eyes burned for a moment on Nikki and she turned quickly away as if to catch something K. R. had said. She saw Elvira catch sight of Jacques and thread her way through the guests to welcome him.

She sensed that he'd removed his outer coat, handing it to a servant, and was coming toward her. With a quick, desperate movement, she seized Colby's arm. "Will the handsomest gentleman here escort me to the dining room?"

"Bet your last dollar!"

At the quietly elegant table, she determined to stay cool and enjoy the meal. Her poise was undermined when Jacques was seated directly across from her with only a gossamer curtain of candlelight between them.

What was wrong with her tonight? Why did that lean, chiseled face appear so devilishly, hypnotically handsome, etched as it was in the candle's glow? His eyes were as black as the night.

The storm, she thought, must have something to do with it. There was a kind of tension, an electricity in the air stirred by the growing ferocity of the elements outside, sensitizing, heightening her awareness.

Her eyes skipped away and she concentrated on small talk with the people on either side of her, K. R. to her left and, on the right, a horse rancher from Spain come to do business at Elmhurst. But her gaze always crept back to the inky fire in Jacques' eyes. Skipped away...almost desperately...came sliding back.

Unwillingly she was drawn to his presence, held by a quirk of his lips, his sip from a wineglass and always his eyes. Silently he was reminding her of those intimacies they shared. He might as well have reached across the table and unsnapped the rhinestone clasps on the shoulders of her dress, letting it fall from her bosom, her breasts rising eagerly to the hunger of his lips. His parted lips re-created the moment of their explorations over her trembling, burning flesh...lips all the way across the table, far removed, but projecting their sensation even as he bent his head slightly to one side to catch some small remark Mrs. Tomkins had made.

Was she forever doomed to be enslaved by a physical desire for this one man? Why, when there were dozens of men who would fight over her if she gave them any encouragement? Was it because Jacques had been the first to awaken her womanhood? Was her body remembering when her reasoning mind struggled to forget? It was as if her emotions longed for what her rational thoughts furiously rejected. The resulting battle had her nerves on screaming edge.

She slipped a glance at the faces down the long table. They were relaxed, aglow with good food, drink and companionship. The quietly animated hum of conversation and occasional laughter reflected the mood of well-being.

The tension was concentrated at her end of the table, the seething undercurrent of sexual awareness and tension, almost palpable, so real that it surely seemed the others around them would detect it.

The way Jacques looked at her, with those burning dark eyes, she knew with uncomfortable certainty that he desired her tonight with as much fire as she felt burning in herself. Love had nothing to do with it, she thought bitterly. Wanting her didn't mean he loved her. Perhaps had never meant he loved her. That she had once loved him, she had no doubt. That the spark might still be there was a possibility she refused to consider.

She arched a brow with all the coolness she could muster. Somehow she had to escape this feeling that he could drag her helplessly, willingly, to some dark hideaway where the night would become as soft as down.

Perhaps talking business would bring back a measure of sanity. She drew a breath, leaned toward him. "Jacques." She managed to speak the name impersonally.

"Yes?"

"How are you finding Crestland?"

"Very comfortable. Why? Should I have a particular reaction?"

She smiled distantly. "I hope you don't get to feeling you can't part with the place."

He gave her a penetrating, thoughtful look, as if trying to read her mind. "I have no present intention of doing that. I have some half-formed plans to bring French stock over and go into American racing on a large scale."

"But with all your other interests, how can you find the time?"

"I can usually manage for the things I want most to do. Such as—" his eyes toyed with her "—accepting Elvira's invitation to dinner this evening."

"I'm sure Elvira is pleased to have you as a guest."

"The pleasure is all mine."

She nibbled a bite of filet mignon. It was exquisitely prepared, but she didn't taste it. "I happen to have plans for Crestland myself," she said bluntly.

He raised an eyebrow. "Oh? You do?"

"Yes," she said firmly. "Crestland was the home of my mother's family, the Jacksons, for generations, ever since the plantation home was first built."

"Yes, I'm aware of that." He nodded.

"My grandfather lost it through a series of misfortunes. I've planned for a long time to buy it back. If I should win the Derby—when I win the Derby—I'll be in a position to talk about a purchase—"

"I doubt that even a Derby purse—"

"I know. I probably know the value of Crestland better than all the real estate brokers in Kentucky. I have additional funds that I've been saving. After the Derby I plan to make a serious offer. I hope you'll consider it."

The light in his eyes changed subtly, brooding on her face. After a little, he said, "You've thought about this for a long time, haven't you?"

"I can't see the relevancy of your question. I'm speaking strictly business. I'd like to know two things. First, would you be willing to sell Crestland at the right price?"

He chuckled. "There are meaner gossips who'd tell you that I'd sell anything—for a profit."

The pretended cynicism of his words rolled off her. She was too well aware of his many charities in Europe. During their brief marriage, she had found out Jacques Trenchard was considered the softest touch on the continent. But charity was the last thing she wanted from Jacques.

"I don't expect you to dispose of a property like Crestland at a loss. My second question is your price."

"Price? But I haven't said I would sell."

Anger brought a flush to her cheeks. "You suggested as much!"

Whatever he might have said next was interrupted by a crash of thunder and the raging noise of the storm sweeping its full fury onto the the house. Windows rattled. Ancient oak timbers creaked.

"Excuse me," Nikki said, arising quickly, everything involving Jacques suddenly wiped from her mind. "I must check on Johnny."

She hurried from the dining room, up the long stairs and down a hall to Johnny's room. When she opened the door, the baby-sitter Nikki had hired for the evening, an elderly neighbor woman, Mrs. Crowly, put her knitting down and moved to Nikki's side. "My, that's some dreadful weather we're having, isn't it?" she asked softly.

"Yes. Johnny...?"

"Sleeping peacefully."

Nikki nodded. "Thank goodness he's such a sound sleeper. Thunderstorms scare him."

She walked to the bed and smiled fondly at the tousled curly head on the pillow. Gently she arranged the covers around his shoulders, bent and gave his cheek a soft kiss. He stirred slightly, then went on with his dream.

"Sleep tight, little boy," she whispered, repeating one of their rituals. "Don't let the bedbugs bite."

"If he wakes up and gets frightened, you be sure to come downstairs and get me," Nikki told Mrs. Crowly.

"I will, Nikki. You go ahead with your party. Johnny and I will be fine here in this snug old house. I guess it's weathered a lot worse storms than this, all the years it's been here."

"I guess." She smiled.

She left and on her return to the dining room, she met Jacques coming up the stairs.

"Is Johnny all right?" he asked, his eyes showing concern.

"Yes, fine," she said shortly. "He sleeps like a rock. I hired a woman to keep him company tonight since I'd be at Elvira's dinner, so he isn't alone."

Jacques nodded, looking relieved.

Not wanting to spend a moment more than was necessary with him on the isolated stairway, she hurried past him to the dining room.

She had hardly gotten seated at the table when the old mansion was suddenly plunged into darkness except for the flickering glow from candles on the table.

A bolt of lightning split apart the heavens outside, illuminating startled faces for a split second like images in a waxworks. A crash of thunder rattled the dishes on the table and deafened ears.

The acrid hint of scorched ozone touched the suddenly oppressive air. Nikki, stiffened in her chair, saw the vague figure of her father rising from the chair at the far end of the table.

He glanced first down the length of the table to where Elvira was seated. He dropped his napkin on the table and said in a quiet, reassuring voice to the guests,

"Please give the back-up generator a moment to kick in. You will have light. Continue with your meal. I need to check things outside. I'll rejoin you shortly!"

In the echo of his words the lights flickered on. With a parting nod and smile of reassurance, Colby was moving toward the kitchen. He was unflustered, moving with deceptive speed. At once, Nikki sensed that he had divined something was very wrong.

She slipped out of her chair and caught up with him as he stepped from the kitchen door out into the storm.

"Oh, good Lord!" she gasped. The awesome power of the night had zeroed in on the majestic old oak at the corner of stable C. The lightning had shattered the towering tree, spraying flaming debris in all directions. Out of the treetop a fiery mass had hurtled onto the roof of the stable. The building was a tinderbox of dry hay and weathered pine plank construction. Already it was spurting skyrockets of devouring fire.

Stark terror chilled the blood in Nikki's veins.

"I glimpsed it from the corner window in the dining room," Colby said. Then he ordered, "Stay in the house, Nikki."

She hardly heard him. She felt nothing of the lashing wind and sting of driving rain. Through the noise of the storm she heard the scream of terrorized horses.

There were three thoroughbreds in stable C. Two of them belonged to Elvira. The third was Banshee.

A thin scream tore from her throat. She saw Colby limned against the unreal surging of firelight, ducking his head, shielding his face with his arm as he dashed closer to the door of the barn.

Nikki hurtled forward. Then a jolt of pain shot through her shoulder as a leanly powerful hand caught her wrist and held her back.

She spun around, seeing Jacques' face through the sheets of rain. "Let me go!" she cried. "Jacques, damn you...let me go."

"Pull yourself together, Nikki. This is no time for hysterics."

She fought him furiously, hammering at him with her fists. From somewhere in the surreal, ghastly scene she heard Orlis' voice shouting at her father.

"They're in there," she sobbed. "My father, Orlis...the horses...Banshee. The place will explode any second...." She tugged, jerked. "I said let me go!"

Jacques glanced at a burly groom, one of the men who had rushed from various directions, clustering in the yard. He shoved Nikki against the groom. "You keep her back! Do you understand? If you don't keep her here, you'll wish you'd walked barefoot into that barn!"

The groom took one look at Jacques' eyes and said, "Yes sir."

Nikki stood helplessly imprisoned in the groom's sturdy grip, watching with horror-filled eyes as geysers of fire spurted from the doomed stable. She heard the scream of a horse, knew it was Banshee and her heart was wrenched from her.

The rain gates opened completely and a torrential downpour was drenching her, plastering the Givenchy to her shivering skin, the hair against her cheek. The downpour made the tongues of flame spurting through the roof hiss and spew steam, but it wasn't reaching the holocaust inside the building. She was unaware of the rain beating against her. Every atom of her being centered on the broad doorway to the smoke-filled stable, where flames spurted hungrily ever lower, touching off dust-mote explosions and more curls of fire.

The groom permitted her a few steps closer to the forefront of the shocked crowd that suddenly reeled back as a roof timber collapsed, sending a fresh tower of fire sizzling and smoking in the rain.

She strained forward from the waist, lips parted but not breathing as she first heard then saw her father leading two terror-crazed horses out into the blessing of the driving rain.

Then she sobbed with joy as Jacques appeared leading Banshee. But suddenly she screamed, "Orlis! Oh, you fool, get out of there!" But he was nowhere to be seen.

She felt the heat. It was pushing the others back. She saw Jacques handing a rearing, wild-eye Banshee over to a pair of grooms.

Jacques bent low, ran to the smoke- and flame-filled doorway. The huge doorway lintel, hewn from a solid log, cracked and bent, spilling sparks in Jacques' pathway.

He fell back, looked about desperately. Nikki went numb all over. She had the nerveless thought—he's picking up that old tarpaulin, throwing it over himself, going back in there....

She lunged, but the groom's massive arm held her back. She squirmed, kicked, but he was unrelenting. Then she fell back against him limply, for the south wall of the barn tilted out and crashed in flaming wreckage. Too late. Jacques...Orlis...

She only wanted to turn away, to go someplace in privacy huddled with the shock and grief. Then she heard the groom cry out, "Look!"

She spun around. Against the canvas of fire, she saw as if in slow-motion a smoking tarpaulin humped up to a height of some four or five feet come staggering out of the raging inferno.

There was a rush into the perimeter of the heat as Jacques cleared the collapsing doorway. Eager hands lifted the charred tarp, revealing a singed Jacques Trenchard with Orlis draped over his shoulder.

Jacques staggered, went to his knees and Orlis fell free, lying on his back as life-giving rain spattered his creased face. His eyes flicked open and caught sight of the faces crowding over him.

"Would you believe," he said, his voice husky from the smoke he'd inhaled, "that I let a horse kick me? Sure as the good Lord made little apples, Orlis Washington lost his footing in a horse barn and let a crazed horse lay one on him!"

His gaze moved to Jacques' face. "Thanks, Mr. Trenchard. Good to know they still grow men in France. I was over there, y'know...in 1944... infantry...."

Jacques patted his shoulder. "Take it easy, Orlis. No need to talk now." He heard the sound of an ambulance. "We'll get you to the hospital now and get some treatment for all the smoke you swallowed."

To Nikki, the events of the night had become hazy. She was dimly aware of Jacques turning to her, taking her from the groom's arms. She was as limp as a rag. Her emotions were tattered. Her consciousness centered on the warm strength of Jacques' arms holding her—without them she would have collapsed.

She felt herself being scooped up, carried into the house up the stairs. She felt numb, almost detached, as if a vague participant in a slow-motion sequence.

Then she was looking up at Jacques' soot-streaked face. Dimly she realized she was on her bed. Her teeth began chattering as a violet chill shook her body.

Jacques' eyes were filled with concern. He disappeared from her view for a moment, then was back, his hands filled with thick towels.

"You're soaked to the bone," he murmured. "We need to get you dry and warm or you're going to get sick."

She protested weakly as he slipped the dress from her shoulder. But the movement of his hands was sure and firm. Her need to be taken care of and protected after tonight's emotionally drained experience was seductively enticing.

Within seconds he had stripped her wet clothes from her body and was rubbing her bare skin briskly with the towels. When she tried to fend off his hands he only chuckled indulgently. "My dear, don't pretend I have never seen you this way before."

Perhaps, but he was obviously enjoying the view now. His dark eyes were growing murky, his breathing swifter.

Her face flushed, Nikki pulled the sheet around her, covering herself. She had stopped shivering. She felt dry and warm—more than warm. Her flesh burned.

"Thank you, I'm all right now."

"Sure?"

"Yes."

He was seated on the edge of the bed, gazing down, his face close.

"Jacques..." she began.

"Yes?"

She gazed directly into his eyes, a sudden wave of emotion making speech difficult. She was overwhelmed with gratitude for what he had done tonight. With no thought of his own safety, he had heroically kept tonight from becoming a horrible tragedy. "Thank you. Thank you, Jacques, for risking your life so gallantly, thank you for saving Orlis...thank you for saving Banshee...."

He smiled, looking at her steadily.

"Next to my father and Johnny," she went on tearfully, "Orlis and Banshee are the most important beings in my life. We're a family."

"Yes, I know," he murmured.

"I don't know what I would have done if they had died in the fire—" She choked, unable to go on.

"But they're all right," he assured her.

"Yes, thanks to your heroism. You ought to have a medal or something."

This time he laughed. "Well, hardly that, I think. I'm glad I happened to be there at the right time."

Nikki swallowed, continuing to gaze at him.

It was a strange moment, out of the context of things, a small segment of time separated from the normal course of events. For just this fraction of existence, she had a flood of feelings for Jacques that belonged only to tonight. Tomorrow morning, no doubt, all the bitterness and estrangement would return. But for the moment, she could only feel engulfed by a wave of gratitude and admiration for this strong man.

She looked straight into his eyes, and he into hers, their gazes reaching deep into one another with a silent communication far more eloquent than words.

His head bent closer. She was only dimly aware of the dying storm outside that tossed handfuls of raindrops against her windowpane in a parting farewell. Her senses became a whirlpool spinning around, sucking her into intense black eyes.

Her arms moved of their own accord, reaching up to encircle his neck. His face bent closer.

She was aware of the blood coursing through her arteries in steady, pounding surges.

Then his lips were on hers, gently at first, questioningly, then, receiving her answer, more fervently, with increasing hunger that she tried to fulfill. Her breath became a sob in her throat. Her body arched as his arm slipped under her and he drew her closer.

"Nikki," he whispered thickly against her closed eyelids, "I meant what I said that night in the restaurant. You are even more desirable than I remembered. You were an adorable girl when I first saw you. Now you have become a seductive woman...."

His lips sought hers again. She met his kiss with an equal eagerness. She wasn't surprised at her response—she had been fighting this desire from the first moment she'd seen him again. Now she was unable to fight any longer. The dam broke, unleashing a surging tidal wave of primitive passion. The kiss shook her to the foundation of her being.

Then a cold wave of fright overcame the fever burning through her veins. She pulled back from him, drawing the sheet more tightly around her. Her eyes were wide, pupils distended. She was shivering again, but this time from fright rather than cold—the fright of knowing how vulnerable she still was to this man who had once broken her heart and was right now demonstrating how easily he could break it again....

Chapter Eleven

In the days that followed, Nikki tried to blot that moment of insanity in Jacques' arms from her mind, blaming it on the near hysterical state into which she had been plunged by the storm and fire.

The dramatic events of the night left Nikki with an emotional hangover. In the cold light of the next morning, despite the return of sanity, Jacques' passionate kiss still burned on her lips. She felt humiliated. How could she have behaved so wantonly with a man she despised? She was furious with herself. And the anger was intensified by recurring waves of desire even now. Just thinking about Jacques' arms around her, the hunger of his lips on hers, their closeness with only a thin sheet protecting her, sent hot waves coursing through her again.

She remembered his searching hands, his caresses under the sheet, seeking remembered, intimate secrets, and the tempo of her heart increased.

With an exclamation, she jumped from the bed and plunged into a cold shower.

Her head cleared; the primitive yearnings were swept away. She could think rationally. She was able to view what had transpired with a sensible perspective. The wrenching drama of the fire and the horror of the near tragedy had thrown her into a state of temporary insanity. Her emotions had run rampant. She could not be held accountable for her actions. She had been overwhelmed with gratitude for Jacques' heroic act. Under the circumstances it was easy to understand her vulnerability. Viewed from that perspective, she could forgive herself for her emotional response to his kiss.

She was truly grateful to him. And he had done a heroic thing. Still, that was no excuse to fall into bed with him. True, they had once been married. They had known one another intimately before. And under the circumstances—since she had been covered only by the filmy sheet and Jacques had been holding her and kissing her—it had been normal to remember the heights of ecstasy to which their lovemaking had once carried her and to yearn for that fulfillment again. But it would have been a fulfillment leaving the bitter ashes of regret in its wake. Jacques would have been the victor, his male ego pleased with his conquest, his physical hunger satisfied. She remembered with wrenching bitterness that he had spoken of how desirable she was—but the word "love" had not passed his lips.

Fortunately she had come out of the dangerous situation with a measure of her self-respect intact. She had avoided fresh heartbreak. For that she was deeply grateful. Now however, she faced the awkward problem of seeing Jacques again. For he would most certainly be back. Now that he had made contact with his son, he was a regular visitor to Elmhurst.

It would take some effort on her part to face him after last night. She would feel self-conscious, embarrassed. Somehow she would keep any conversation between them formal and distant. She would make it icily clear that what had happened between them last night had been a temporary aberration. She would offer nothing further for his ego to feed on!

She had plenty to keep her busy, to keep her mind off the emotional turmoil Jacques Trenchard could cause her. Her life became a montage of rushing hours, always too few in a single day. She was at the training track, discovering how rapidly her leg restored itself, refining her riding technique.

Orlis was back from the hospital, completely recovered from the effects of the fire and on hand at the track when she trained. "Too much face up in the slipstream," Orlis noted. "Bad aerodynamics."

Or Colby: "Overcorrection. Keep your backside down. Your back should be parallel to the horse's."

Or sometimes an exchange between Orlis and Colby.

"Pretty good ride that time. She looked like the old Nikki Cameron, didn't she, Orlis?"

"Well...almost, Mr. Cameron. There's still something missing...can't quite put my finger on it...."

An added onus in the comeback training was the surrender of Banshee's saddle to other jockeys. It was mutually agreed that someone else would ride Banshee in the early preliminary races until Nikki had made a full recovery.

Whenever Banshee and Colby were off to the prestigious meets—the only kind that qualified a horse for the Derby—Nikki would have the singeing memory of Gulfstream and how it had determined her course in this all-important year when Banshee was a three-year-old. She thought bitterly that she should be in Banshee's saddle.

Nikki had been temporarily away from Elmhurst three years ago when, at the usual ungodly wee-morning hour, Lady Camellia had foaled Banshee by Blue Thunder. The birth occured on January 10, which gave Banshee a developmental head start on most thoroughbreds born that year. Since all foals are designated "yearlings" on January 1 of the year following their birth regardless of the actual birthdate, Banshee had an edge on other yearlings born later in the year.

As Banshee weaned and tested his first legs, Colby crossed his fingers and murmured a prayer. The colt was the most perfect produced at Elmhurst to date. His conformation was classic. His bloodlines were traceable to the three Eastern—Barb and Arabian—stallions from whom all thoroughbreds in America were diversely descended: the Darley Arabian, Byerly Turk and the Godolphin Barb. And Banshee was from the small portion of Elmhurst stock owned exclusively by Colby Cameron.

Colby had registered the pedigree showing joint ownership by himself and his daughter, Nikki.

Nikki loved the big, handsome brute and he loved her in an animal-human rapport that was uncanny. Colby swore that half the time Banshee understood what Nikki was saying.

Colby took personal charge of Banshee, his heart beating a little faster from the moment of the first time clockings. He dared voice a prediction to himself. "This one isn't just a winner. This one is a Kentucky Derby champion...a Hall of Famer, a model for another proud statue someday in a Lexington park...."

While Colby thought of Derby day in the third official year of Banshee's life, Nikki couldn't stop her mind from spinning a fantasy of its own. She trained with Banshee at every opportunity. She had never ridden such a horse. A Derby win—the Run for the Roses. She and Banshee in the winner's circle, a master of ceremonies bringing Elvira and Colby into the range of national television cameras...the presentation for the coveted horseshoe of roses.

And the biggest prize of all—Crestland!

That's what it could amount to. A Derby purse plus the carefully hoarded savings of her riding career could put her in a bargaining position for Crestland. But would Jacques sell? The answer to that question had been interrupted by the fire the night of the storm. It was a question that had to be asked again, and she would at the earliest opportunity.

Nikki rode to her own private hilltop to gaze across the rolling acres of Crestland. She shivered with the thought that its return to her ownership could actually happen. With hard work, with horse and human sweat, with just a little luck—and wasn't all life shaped by strokes of luck? And wasn't luck, despite all the variables that shaped it, something you could help determine for yourself?

There were the precarious bridges to cross: the prep races; the competition, with more than four hundred other nominations from which the field would be drawn.

Being a tough realist, Nikki refused to quake before the odds. She had confidence in Banshee. Somebody won that crown jewel of American races every May. Somebody was handed that winner's net of about three-quarters of a million dollars plus the future fabulous spin-offs in stud fees and yearlings sales. Tough realist, she accepted the odds because she knew the truth of Banshee and herself.

They had a chance and neither she nor Banshee wanted more than an equal shot. She, together with Orlis and Colby, knew the unrevealed fact that she could get about three-hundredths of a second more speed from Banshee over the distance than any other jockey.

Her career had brought her to the rarefied realms at Aqueduct, Belmont, Santa Anita. Then Gulfstream....

And now, because of Gulfstream, she'd been forced to watch some of the early qualifying races from the sidelines while other jockeys rode Banshee—jockeys who were competent but who lacked the rapport with the big stallion that she alone possessed.

"It's best this way for now, honey," Colby pointed out. "I can get Dinki Dillman for Banshee. He's a good jockey."

"I should be riding Banshee," Nikki said bitterly.

"And you will be, honey," he promised. "But first some other mounts for you until you're back in your old form."

He was being tactful, Nikki thought. He was avoiding the truth—better play it safe with a competent, adequate jockey on Banshee for the present, a jockey who wasn't recovering from a near fatal spill. He might not get that last ounce of speed out of the big black stallion with the white star and white stockings, the way Nikki could when she was in top form, but he'd run a good race. Right now, Nikki was still a question mark in everyone's minds. In her own mind, for that matter!

Too important to risk everything by having Nikki blow up, her nerves coming unglued somewhere in a crowded field.

While Dinky Dillman was off riding Banshee in the prepping races, Nikki began her comeback elsewhere. She was at Charles Town, for her first track competition since Gulfstream, riding a claimer, fighting back

the Gulfstream accident, and she won easily. She was at
Oldsmar, pretending that the Gulfstream spill hadn't
really happened, giving an all-male handicap field a
taste of mud from her horse's heels.

The sportswriters were taking note:

GIRL JOCKEY MAKING COMEBACK AFTER NEAR FATAL FALL

Nikki Cameron, glamorous lady jock, who almost lost her life in a bad spill at Gulfstream ear-
lier this year, showed some of her old fire today,
giving the male competition a fit.

All very encouraging, except for that hidden gnaw-
ing doubt deep within that she kept to herself.

She was at Aqueduct, not lifting the lid on the Gulfstream Pandora's box. Back in the big time, she
thought, but living with the bitter knowledge that
someone else was riding her beloved Banshee.

Back in the big time, yes, but not quite with the edge,
knowing it was back to the old drawing board, knowing that she had run second on a possible winner. She
rode three races that day and was fretful as she changed
out of her silks. Something was not quite right, and she
kept reviewing her rides during a sleepless night, hoofbeat by hoofbeat. Technically, she'd been among the
cream of the jockeys in the field. But a nagging feeling
of wrongness refused to go away. She had lost a challenge by a nose, failed to get full response from her

mount in a second race. Why? She was doing every-thing right. Yet, in standing aside and looking at her-self mercilessly, she was reminded of the violinist or pianist whose technical skills are honed to perfection but who nevertheless isn't a virtuoso. How to account for it?

One thing was sure: only virtuosity would make the Run for the Roses, horses and jockeys alike. At least Banshee was hitting his stride in the big stakes events. Nikki dared a first grain of certainty that the big stal-lion was going to be drawn from the scores of nomina-tions for the starting field of twenty, cream of the cream. But when the steward called, "Jockeys up," who would it be? It must be she! Prior to Gulfstream she'd always gotten that extra three-hundredths of a second out of Banshee. And in the supreme test for three-year-olds at a grueling mile and one-quarter, three-hundredths of a second had vital meaning.

Jacques rode over during that montage of days to play with his son and occasionally watch Nikki train.

"I'm spying for the competition," he would say laughing. It was no secret that he had his own entry planned for the Derby, a beautiful chestnut mare named Le Cheval. The Horse. What arrogant simplicity, Nikki thought, trying not to be so painfully aware of his presence. Nevertheless she wished he wouldn't come around when she was training. Just knowing he was watching made her self-conscious and threw her timing off.

She tried to avoid personal contact with him. The times she couldn't avoid speaking with him, she had kept the conversation politely distant. He had responded with an amused half smile, but the expression in his eyes made it clear that he hadn't forgotten that moment of intimacy. While his conversation was about horses or about an afternoon he planned to spend with Johnny, his eyes raked her with a bold, brazen look that made her face burn.

One Sunday midday, about the time Nikki, Johnny and Elvira returned from church service, the Crestland station wagon appeared in the driveway.

A lanky young groom dressed in his best Sunday dark suit got out of the driver's seat. "Message for Miss Nikki Cameron," he announced.

Nikki crossed to the parked wagon while Elvira and Johnny, giving the wagon a questioning glance, went into the house.

Nikki took the proffered envelope and tore open the flap with its embossed Crestland seal.

She unfolded the note and read, *May I have the pleasure of your company this evening for dinner at Antoine's? Jacques.*

A half smile tugged at her lips. The formal gesture of the note reminded her of the first time Jacques had invited her to dinner, in the horse barn at Keeneland. How romantic and dashing that had seemed to her young heart at the time!

Now she glanced up at the groom with a puzzled frown. "Antoine's? There isn't any Antoine's around here. Surely he doesn't mean the Antoine's in New Orleans.''

The groom laughed. ''I guess he does, ma'am. The boss can mean anything. He said with your kind permission I am to bring you to Crestland.''

''Now?'' she asked incredulously.

''The minute you kindly accept the invitation. He said the Lear is fueled and he's giving it a final check. He said to mention that whatever you wore to church would be suitable for the occasion.''

Nikki glanced down at herself. She was hardly in dungarees. The soft blue walking suit, nylons, shoes with dressy high heels, white silk blouse and silver earrings beaten in a tiny pattern of dogwood leaves to match the pin on her lapel wouldn't bar the door at Antoine's or any other place.

She chewed her lip in a moment of painful indecision. Why would he possibly want to go to the extent of flying her to New Orleans for dinner? What did he have up his sleeve? A continuation of the kiss that night of the fire? Warning bells went off in her mind. She remembered how passionately he had kissed her, his husky voice whispering how desirable she was. No mention of love. Just desire.

Perhaps, she thought, to a man with his reputation for romantic conquests, there was some kind of special challenge to his swollen male ego to see if he could seduce his ex-wife back into bed with him.

Or did it have something to do with Johnny? Or Crestland?

The questions tumbled uneasily through her mind. She did want to discuss the matter of her buying Crestland, and a dinner setting would be fine for that. But flying to Antoine's in a Lear jet? Wasn't that overdoing it just a bit? Then again, to a man like Jacques Trenchard, whose home was the entire world, it was probably no more than a trip to the corner delicatessen.

She chose to ignore the warning signals in her mind in favor of the gathering excitement at such a glamorous invitation.

"Well, all right, then." She slowly nodded, despite her misgivings. "Wait just a moment while I let them know in the house where I'm off to."

Less than half an hour later, the Lear needled its way from the Crestland airstrip to the reaches of a blue sky, where little puffs of cottony white cumulus here and there hung like Christmas decorations. Nikki watched a cloud mist slither past the cabin window while her body felt the sensation of G-pressure as the plane jetted to flight altitude.

She stole a glance at Jacques in the pilot's seat. He was all business flying the plane, his features a study in concentration as he gave the instruments and controls his full attention. He's a fine pilot, she had to admit to herself. He gave her a feeling of confidence and safety. But then he always had. His strength and masculine assertiveness made her feel he could protect her under any circumstances, could cope with any threat. From the outside, that is. The real danger, the real threat, was from inside.

His profile was so handsome. She felt a catch in her throat, forced herself to look away, to stare at the limitless blue depths as they burst out of the cloud.

He leveled off, set the auto and stirred in his seat.

"Close to lunchtime." He smiled. "How about a sandwich from the picnic hamper and something cold to drink?"

Lunch in space. Caviar. Imported cheeses. Champagne, of course. Later, dinner at Antoine's. She burst into impulsive laughter. "I should have known about you from that experience of having a dinner catered in a Keeneland yearling barn!"

"Then you remember?"

"Of course. How could a girl that age forget such an absolutely insane experience? I was little more than a teenager." She said it with a half-accusing tone. What chance did she have—inexperienced as she was in the way of worldly, sophisticated men—against Jacques Trenchard?

"It was crazy, perhaps, but a happy event. Such as being here with you now, high in the heavens with the earth far below."

You can forget the smooth lines, my chivalrous French Don Juan, she thought, all her defenses fully operational.

"That sounds quite rehearsed," she murmured cynically. "I suppose it's standard procedure for ladies carried off in the Lear. I would imagine a long line of young women have preceded me in this seat."

He gave her an impatient glance. "Surely you don't believe all that foolish gossip printed by the tabloids?"

She shrugged breezily. "Some exaggeration, perhaps..."

"A lot of exaggeration," he snorted. "If a fourth of those stories were true, I'd have no time left for business at all."

She smiled, knowing she had insinuated a wrong mood into the moment, a mood he hadn't planned, didn't want. She'd sounded petty and that went against her grain. But now that she was actually here, her reactions suddenly had an untrustworthy shimmer. In this isolation, this being alone with him so close and everything else so far away....

Again she felt that traitorous stirring of emotions, the yearning for this kind of instant. Merely his presence suffused a day already lovely in its own right. The Lear was a silver lance shooting her into realms untouched, causing her blood to stir more quickly.

She wasn't sure her defenses would be able to stand up to the mood he could create if left entirely to his own devices. She could feel the thickening of her breath, the prickling awareness of her garments against her flesh. She became conscious of her own body. Her breasts had grown full and aching against her bra, which seemed suddenly too small. All of it was a sensitivity to the gathering desire that being isolated like this with him could awaken. His body seemed to give off vibrations of heat and electricity that made the very air tingle.

Grasping for a fresh hold on defense, she said, "I'm sure the stories about Gina Anotia are not exaggerated."

He glanced at her again with a look that was half-speculative, half-amused. "Do I detect a hint of jealousy?"

"Certainly not!" she exclaimed indignantly.

"But it disturbs you that the media has linked me romantically with Gina."

"It does not!"

"Sounds as if the lady doth protest too much!" He chuckled.

Nikki felt her cheeks growing hot. She wanted desperately to change the subject. "I have absolutely no interest in your romantic affairs, Jacques. What I would like to know is exactly what got into that devious head of yours to talk to me into this insane dinner date?"

"I have something important to discuss with you. Antoine's struck me as an ideal place to do it."

She gave him a closer, narrow-eyed look. "Discuss what?"

"We'll go into that over dinner."

She was burning with curiosity, but he refused to add any more to what he had said.

She wondered if it was the altitude or the champagne that was giving her a giddy, reckless feeling. Couldn't be the altitude, she thought. The cabin was pressurized. Blame it on the champagne? But she'd only had one glass....

They landed in New Orleans too early for dinner, so Jacques rented a car. They drove past the great Superdome, down the vast width of Canal Street and turned onto one of the narrow, cobblestone streets of the Vieux Carré, the old French Quarter of the city.

Suddenly Nikki felt transported back in time, to an era of gaslights and horse-drawn carriages. In fact, Jacques rented just such a carriage operated by a man dressed in an eighteenth-century livery costume, and they clip-clopped down the streets.

"Ah, what a fine old city," Jacques exclaimed with delight. "One of my favorites. You Americans don't do enough to preserve this kind of charm. You have the mistaken notion that everything has to be new, shiny, full of chrome and glass, higher and bigger. Look around us, those ancient courtyards, the lovely iron filigree around the balconies—they have the mellow softness that only comes from age."

Nikki settled back in the carriage smiling as Jacques rattled on enthusiastically. She said, "I don't understand you. You've been everywhere. You've seen the pyramids, gone mountain climbing in India, shopped in Singapore. Seems like all the cities would look alike after a while."

"Oh, no!" he protested. "Each is unique. Each has its own personality like a lovely woman. This old section is like a fine wine that has taken more than a century to give it its flavor. Have you been to New Orleans before?"

"Briefly. I have the feeling I'm seeing it for the first time, though."

The carriage brought them back to Jackson Square as the shadows were lengthening. It was a warm, peaceful late Sunday afternoon. Couples sat on benches or sprawled on the grass of the park near the statue of Andrew Jackson on horseback. Pigeons trundled along the pathways cooing and fluttering from underfoot. On the nearby Mississippi, a tugboat hooted like a big, impatient owl.

Slowly they crossed the park, then strolled around its perimeter. It was an area alive with every color of the rainbow, bright reds, pastel blues, vivid greens, all splashed on artists' canvases hung along the iron fence that bordered the park. They paused before an artist who did quick charcoal sketches for a fee. Over Nikki's protests, Jacques instructed the man to do a drawing of her.

"Draw her beside a horse," Jacques ordered. "A black horse with a white star on his forehead. That will keep her in character."

She laughed self-consciously when the artist completed his sketch and swung it around for her to see. It made her look like a movie starlet.

"Looks just like you," Jacques said as they strolled away. He carried the drawing under one arm.

"Don't be ridiculous. The man makes his living by flattering his subjects. The rascal is an artistic con man. The horse looks realistic, though."

They paused on a corner and listened to a street band, a group consisting of a battered trumpet, banjo and washboard playing a barely recognizable version of a traditional Dixieland melody.

They strolled down Royal Street, looking at antiques in the windows. They had cocktails in a courtyard surrounded by great banana trees.

As darkness fell over the city, the gaslights on Bourbon Street's corners glowed and the happy sound of Dixieland jazz floated from doorways.

"How's your appetite?" Jacques asked.

"This sight-seeing has me starved."

"Good! We are about to enjoy dinner at one of the finest restaurants in the world. That's something for a Frenchman to admit."

"You probably only do that because this city was once a French colony and the menu at Antoine's is in French."

He laughed. "Touché."

Antoine's. Seven thirteen St. Louis Street, in the heart of the French Quarter. It had been an American institution since its inception in 1840.

"Are you familiar with Antoine's?" Jacques asked.

"Everybody knows about Antoine's. It was even used as the setting for a mystery novel, *Dinner at Antoine's.*"

"Then I made the right kind of reservation for us—in the Mystery Room. It's a special room for special people, limited to a few tables, a gourmet's sanctum unequaled anywhere else in the country."

Of course, she thought. That would suit his style.

He went on to talk about the celebrities who had eaten at Antoine's: both Roosevelts, Teddy and Franklin; Calvin Coolidge; the explorer Admiral Byrd; the World War I French general, Marshal Foch; Will Rogers; Ernest Hemingway...the list went on and on. The walls were covered with their photographs.

Seated amidst the mellow decor, Nikki and Jacques were introduced to their waiter for the evening, LeMoines. While the busboy stood at LeMoines' side, Jacques spoke rapidly in French.

The tuxedoed waiter clicked his heels and gave Nikki a short bow. "We are indeed honored, Madame Trenchard."

What kind of hogwash had Jacques conveyed in his mother tongue? The rat! Madame Trenchard indeed! "Madame Trenchard" had existed only during the delirium of a too hasty marriage and too brief honeymoon in France; that was all.

"What would be Madame Trenchard's delight for dinner tonight?" Jacques asked.

Her cheeks pink, Nikki muttered under her breath, "Jacques, cut out the Madame Trenchard bit. What's gotten into you, anyway?"

He shrugged. "Perhaps it's the mood of the afternoon and evening. It took me back to our honeymoon in Paris."

The pink in Nikki's cheeks grew deeper. She tried not to admit it, but it had been a lovely afternoon and she had enjoyed his company. And why not? Jacques Trenchard was one of the most charming men on the face of the earth. She would have to be comatose not to fall under the spell of that fatal Trenchard charm.

Turning to the menu, she said, "Why don't I have the world-famous specialty, oysters Rockefeller? Wasn't it Antoine's who invented the dish?" she asked the waiter.

"Indeed, madame. In 1889." LeMoines smiled, pleased that she knew the fact. "And since then we have given remembrance cards numbered in sequence with each order of oysters Rockefeller."

"Really?" she asked in surprise. "Must be quite a few by now."

The waiter smiled in delight at Nikki's natural enthusiasm. "Madame, should you order oysters Rockefeller this evening, your personal card will be numbered in the three million-plus range."

"That's quite a lot of oysters!" Nikki exclaimed.

LeMoine relaxed his austere professionalism to give vent to spontaneous laughter at Nikki's expression. "Madame, forgive the forwardness, but I have to say that you are an absolute delight."

"Yes, isn't she?" Jacques agreed.

After the waiter left, Nikki said, "Now do you mind clearing up the mystery of why you flew me all the way down here? You said you had something important to talk to me about and you've been dodging any explanation all afternoon."

"Indeed I do, but it can wait until dessert."

More stalling! Impatiently Nikki said, "Well, then, I have something to talk to you about. I brought up the subject at Elvira's dinner and we were interrupted by the storm. I want to know if you'll consider selling Crestland?''

He smiled wryly. ''You're a typical American, Nikki. All business. Why not relax and enjoy the meal first? We can talk about all that later.''

Nikki experienced a fresh wave of exasperation and frustration, but it was swept aside by the sudden reappearance of the waiter carrying a long box. ''This was delivered at the door for madame,'' he explained with a short bow, placing it in her arms.

Bewildered, Nikki opened the box and gasped at the sight of a dozen beautiful long-stemmed roses. She stared wide-eyed at Jacques. ''Why—'' she spluttered.

Jacques merely smiled. ''Just a small gesture to thank you for the pleasure of your company this evening.''

Nikki experienced a variety of emotions as she looked from Jacques to the beautiful roses. Jacques knew she loved flowers. But why would he have such a costly box of roses delivered to her here? Why the flight down here? Why this romantic dinner setting? He was after something—what was it? Her delight over the flowers was tempered by an undercurrent of wary suspicion. The bitter experience of the past had left her with the feeling that Jacques Trenchard was not to be trusted.

The delicious meal arrived, served with impeccable skill by their waiter. As they savored the exquisite dishes, Jacques said, ''Johnny and I had a great time last week when I took him to see the baseball game.''

''Yes, I know. He talked about it all week.''

"That's quite a son we have, Nikki. Polite, intelligent, inquisitive. You've done a marvelous job of raising him."

Nikki gave Jacques' face a studied look. She saw the warmth and pride that glowed when he spoke about Johnny. Again suspicion stirred in her. Was all this leading to something he was cooking up that involved her son?

She had mixed feelings about the close bond that was developing between Johnny and his father. It made her uneasy. She also felt a slight pang of irrational jealousy. She and Johnny had been so close before Jacques came back into their lives. Yet there were the masculine things a boy could only share with his father. Where would it lead? Was Jacques going to demand more of Johnny's time?

She asked, "Is Johnny the reason you brought me here? Is this what you wanted to talk about?"

"In a way."

Dessert had arrived. Jacques selected a French pastry and café noir. Nikki chose a cup of strong New Orleans coffee laced with chicory.

"If you've gotten some wild notion of taking Johnny off to Europe, you can just forget it," Nikki said coldly.

He held up both hands in a conciliatory gesture. "Nothing like that." Light flashed on the heavy gold ring he wore as he raised his cup for a sip. Putting down the cup, he gave Nikki a long, studied look, then cleared his throat. "What I had in mind was our getting married again."

Chapter Twelve

Nikki remained in a state of numbed shock on the entire flight back to Crestland. She was using all her reasoning ability to sort out tonight's stunning development. There was something totally unreal about the entire day, the flight to New Orleans, the romantic atmosphere of the old French Quarter, the fabulous meal at Antoine's, the flowers and then the climax: Jacques' incredible proposal. Was this all some kind of crazy dream or hallucination from which she would awaken?

At first she hadn't believed he was serious. She was well aware that Jacques's outrageous sense of humor could take such bizarre twists as having dinner catered in a Keeneland horse barn. But no, he had insisted, his eyes grave, he was dead serious.

"Please think it over, Nikki," he had pleaded. "Don't give it a hasty answer."

She could hardly give it an answer at all when she still couldn't believe the question. "Will you marry me again?" The words played over and over in her mind like a recorded tape. Jacques wanting to remarry her? It was simply incredible. Why, after the bitter ending of their hasty marriage? Why, after all these years? Why, why, why?

Her mind was pounding with the question. It was a monumental riddle to which there seemed no reasonable answer.

Her thoughts kept returning to Johnny. That was the only thing that made sense. Jacques was wild about the boy. Would he go so far as to remarry Nikki in order to gain stronger custody of his son? He insisted that wasn't the case, but she couldn't trust him. After the way he'd once rejected her, she doubted she could ever entirely trust him again.

It was near midnight when the Lear swept down to a smooth landing on the Crestland runway. Jacques' employees ran out from the hangar to take care of the plane. "Let's get my car keys and I'll drive you to Elmhurst," Jacques said, escorting Nikki to the house.

A fresh storm of emotions engulfed her as they approached the beautiful old plantation mansion. It gleamed like a jeweled setting in the moonlight. A hurting lump filled her throat. Tears blurred her eyes. She was swept with a wave of homesickness that was unbearable. This should be her home. She should be coming home here tonight.

She had not set foot inside the home since she'd left more than ten years ago, an angry, heartbroken teenager. Since then she'd seen it only from a distance. Now she walked with Jacques between the stately columns, across the wide front porch. Then she was inside, surrounded by the gleam of polished oak hallways, the splendor of mahogany walls. Crystal chandeliers sparkled overhead, darting lights and shadows around the classic molding and cornices.

Many of the antique furnishings had remained, part of the original sale when the house had gone on the auction block. With loving hands, Nikki touched familiar chairs where her mother and grandfather had sat. The chairs, tables, sideboards, china cabinets were hand-crafted masterpieces of colonial cabinetmakers.

Hardly aware of Jacques, she wandered on a nostalgic tour from room to room, through the great library, the stately formal dining room, down the hall and at last to the bedroom that had been hers. She gave a little cry of pleasure at the sight of her old canopied bed. She remembered her toy box that had stood against the east wall. It was still there. And the great windows were there, overlooking the rolling hillside crisscrossed with white rail fences. How she had loved the warm summer nights when breezes had stirred the curtains at those windows, bringing the perfume of Confederate jasmine and the song of the nightingale. Very little had changed.

She turned, suddenly aware of Jacques' presence. He had followed her quietly, not disturbing her mood with words. "You've—you've taken good care of my home," she said gratefully.

His eyes were dark with an inner blaze. "Then marry me and make it your home again," he said, taking her into his arms.

To become the mistress of Crestland again. How tempting! "It would almost be worth it." She smiled wryly.

"Would it be such a sacrifice?" he asked, the smoldering intensity in his eyes holding her captive.

She shook her head slowly. "I—I don't know if I could ever feel the same about you again, Jacques. You killed the love I had for you when you walked out on me six years ago."

His dark-eyed gaze plunged deeply into her. "I can't quite believe that, Nikki. The night of the storm, the fire. When I carried you to your bedroom. The way you kissed me. It was the kiss of a passionate woman being held by a man she desired—"

Nikki's cheeks burned. "Passion and lust are not quite the same as love."

"As you Americans say, don't knock it. There is a powerful attraction between us, Nikki. I feel it. You feel it. Don't deny it."

"I—I can't deny it," she replied weakly. Even now she felt the rising heat of desire, the magnetic pull of her body to his. She felt the throbbing of her flesh, the fullness of her breasts, the hunger for his touch. Yes, the fire was still there, smoldering coals that could burst into flames at his look, his touch....

She pressed her palms against her cheeks. "I—I can't think rationally when you talk like that. Please don't—"

But he was not going to let her go that easily. He drew her closer. His voice was low, making her heart pound. "Imagine it now, Nikki. Remember that dinner in Paris, on our honeymoon, when we left the table to hurry to our room. Remember standing before me, letting your clothes slip to the floor. Remember coming into my arms naked, the contact of our bare flesh—"

"Stop it!" she sobbed.

But he seized the moment to kiss her, a passionate, demanding kiss that shook her to the depths of her being. Her breath became a sobbing gasp. His kisses rained down her throat as her head fell backward. She gasped as he opened her blouse, as his hand slipped under her bra and cupped her throbbing breast.

She heard him from a distance whispering her name. "Nikki...Nikki...."

Her body pressed closer to his, eager for the feel of his strength, his muscles, his hard masculinity.

Then, shaking and weak, she tore herself from his arms, closing her blouse with trembling fingers. "Jacques, going to bed with you now isn't going to solve anything. You have to give me time to think, to sort this all out. I don't know why you want to marry me."

"Because I care for you. Because I want you for my wife."

"I'm not sure that I believe you. I—I have to have time to think. The things that drove us apart in the first place haven't changed. We're still the same two people—"

"No we're not. You were a mere child then. Now you're a woman...a very desirable woman, I must add.

And I, too, have changed, Nikki. I regret things I said...and did. People change. You must believe that. The couple who married so hastily six years ago were two other people."

"I'm not convinced," she said, slowly shaking her head. The basic conflicts between them remained unresolved.

"Nikki," he went on, "you can't make me believe you didn't enjoy this afternoon with me. I think we should become a family again, you, Johnny and me."

The old hurt and bitterness were seeping back as she got her shocked thoughts under control. "How about those awful things you said the day you walked out on me—accusing me of having an affair with Brad Hall!"

He sighed, his eyes clouding. "I've regretted that many times, Nikki. I was hurt, out of my mind with jealousy. You must admit that I had every reason—"

She nodded guiltily. "Yes, Jacques, I'll accept my part of the blame for that. I admit I did use Brad as a defense against you at first. I didn't want to get married, so I told you I was involved with Brad. It wasn't true, but I made it sound as if we were lovers just to make you angry enough to leave me alone. I was afraid of you, afraid of how you were going to change my life. Then you swept me off my feet anyway. But that time you walked in and found Brad in my bedroom—it was completely innocent. There was nothing between Brad and me. We were never more than friends. But you never gave me the chance to explain—"

He held up his hands again. "Nikki, that's all in the past. I'm truly sorry. I believe you. Can we put it behind us?"

Nikki was silent, struggling with this overwhelming turn of events. It was true that the old flame still burned. She could feel it now, the chemistry between them, the electric charge that made her feel alive in his presence, the excitement that churned through her, the yearning hunger she felt at his touch, his look...the sight of him....

"The main thing that drove us apart hasn't changed," she pointed out. "My racing. I know if I were to marry you again we'd have the same conflict over my racing career. In fact, it was the main reason our marriage got in trouble. Brad Hall was just the last straw. You'd expect—no, you'd demand—that I give up racing and devote my life to being the proper wife of a French aristocrat."

She saw a frown cross Jacques' face. "Nikki, you came within a hair of being killed at Gulfstream. Haven't you had just about enough of it?"

She felt a familiar surge of resentment. "You haven't changed, have you? You still want to dictate my life!"

A flush of anger tinged his cheeks. "I've watched you training. I know a few things about horses and riders. That accident at Gulfstream took something out of you, Nikki."

"That's a lie!" she cried furiously.

"No, it's true. It's happened to other jockeys. You don't want to admit it, but I can see it. Something is missing now. You could find yourself in real trouble in a crowded backstretch when a jockey needs that extra ounce of daring." He leaned forward, his eyes intense. "Nikki, hang it up now while there's time. You've proven your point, that you can be a winner in a tough, competitive profession. Don't push your luck."

"That's not it at all!" she fumed. "You're using all that to twist things around so you can run my life the way you want it. I'm supposed to be your proper European wife, the mistress of your home, entertaining your friends, raising your children. Those were the terms you wanted me on the first time and you haven't changed."

A muscle in his jaw knotted. "It's true you couldn't be much of a wife or mother if the next accident you have on a track leaves you in a wheelchair paralyzed from the neck down!"

Nikki put her hands over her ears. "I won't listen to any more of this!" she sobbed.

There was a moment of strained silence. Jacques sighed heavily. "I'm sorry. I didn't intend for the evening to end with a quarrel. We'll drop the subject for now. All right?"

She felt emotionally drained. "I—I don't want to talk about it any more tonight," she agreed. "Take me home, please, Jacques. My mind is in a fog. I can't think or act rationally. This has been an exhausting day."

"Very well. I'm not going to put pressure on you, Nikki. But I'm not giving up easily, either, let me warn you. I'm convinced it would be best for us all—for you, for me, and especially for Johnny—to be a family again."

Would it be best for Johnny? That was part of her dilemma. She was no longer an impulsive teenager, dashing off to France to marry a handsome, debonair stranger who had swept her off her feet. Her life was no longer entirely her own. Decisions that affected her life also affected her son's.

Her eyes felt gritty when she opened them the next morning. She was briefly startled by the suffusion of sunlight into her room. Her sleep had been restless, riddled with disjointed dreams. Nikki summoned energy to fight against the grip of the tired feeling that flowed through her. Resolutely she turned her mind to the arrangement of a busy schedule for the day, fighting back thoughts of that moment when she'd been on the verge of letting the new owner of Crestland make love to her—and tried not to succumb to regret for not having at least the compensating memory of the sexual fulfillment she knew she would have had in Jacques' arms.

She was going to need a clear head to give this proposal of his a lot of thought.

Showered, neat in brushed-denim slacks and jacket, hair drawn into a tight cap and held by a jade clasp at the nape of her neck, she stepped from her room and heard Johnny's laughter down the hallway.

The starting note of the day was exactly right, breakfast with her son in the comfortable warmth of the big Elmhurst kitchen. The lassitude from lack of sleep and emotional residue gradually melted away before her natural energies and the onrush of events. So much remained to be done before Derby day. How could she make a reasonable decision about Jacques's proposal at a time like this? It would have to wait until after she had run the Derby.

At midmorning she was in the office talking on the phone with Colby. Her father was in Florida, where Banshee had won an important stakes race yesterday.

"He's going to be ready," Colby said in a voice clear of doubt.

"And so will I," she said, taking an oath more to herself than to Colby.

"We only have a few more events, Nikki." He was reminding her of the amount of time she had left to make good on her promise.

Her mind flicked over the races she had ridden since her accident. Her leg, she knew, was as good as new. Her physical condition was superb. Her innate talent and experience were equal to that of any of the other jockeys in the claiming and maiden events.

She felt less comfortable when she reviewed the record of those races of the past few weeks. It was not as good as it could have been—a place instead of a win, a nose out when it should have been a win by two lengths, an also-ran on a horse that had borrowed some negative vibes from her when a gap had closed and boxed him in.

But, she reassured herself, her performances hadn't been shadowed by any haunting ghost of that Gulfstream moment of terror. She was not afraid! Definitely, positively. She had shut Gulfstream completely out of her mind.

So why question her comeback record? It was something the sports page writers were talking about with increasing enthusiasm. If they were handing her plaudits, why not accept what they said? They were savagely perceptive, those people. Any visible evidence of the mark of Gulfstream would have been quickly noted and mercilessly written about.

Then why this tiny inner qualm? This minute, nagging, irrational thought that even the experts can be wrong?

She touched her tongue to lips that felt dry. "I'll be ready," she repeated sternly. "Forget the odds makers. And never mind the predictions that Walleyed Wally is a sure thing. We are going to win the Derby this year!"

"That's the confidence we need," Colby agreed.

"Then it's time you put me in Banshee's saddle again," she said firmly. "I know I'm ready. I want to ride him the next time he races."

A surprising development that afternoon temporarily took her mind off her racing. She spent several hours at the country club tennis courts, relaxing with friends. As they were returning to the dressing rooms, she noticed a small crowd gathering around a poolside table.

"What's going on?" she asked.

Ginny Sanders, her tennis partner, swung her racket over her shoulder, grinning. "Autograph hounds, I guess. We don't have an international movie star using the club swimming pool very often."

"Movie star?" Nikki asked blankly.

"Yes. The Italian actress, Gina Anotia."

For a moment Nikki was too stunned to make a reply. Then she stammered, "Gina Anotia? What on earth is—is she doing here?"

"House guest at Crestland, I heard. Flew in from Italy last night."

Then Ginny shot Nikki a concerned glance. "I—I hope I haven't said the wrong thing."

Nikki somehow managed to cover her agitation. "Of course not." She shrugged. "What possible difference could it make to me?"

"Well, I know you and Jacques Trenchard were...well—"

"Married. Yes, quite a few years ago. It was one of those hasty teenage things. The marriage only lasted a few weeks. It was over long ago. Jacques Trenchard means absolutely nothing to me now. If he wants to entertain his mistress here, I certainly couldn't care less!"

With that, she angrily hurried to the locker room. In the shower, the spray of water mingled with the tears of rage that spilled down her cheeks. Right now, she thought, she could cheerfully kill Jacques Trenchard.

The gall of the man! All that phony sincerity the night they flew to New Orleans. "I want you for my wife, Nikki. We should be a family again, you and Johnny and me. I care for you..."

And the whole time he probably had the staff at Crestland preparing for the arrival of his glamorous mistress!

Humiliation scorched her cheeks. She had almost bought his line! She had allowed her passion for him to burst into flames. She had come within an inch of going to bed with him. What a despicable rat he was! She'd been right all along. He'd probably thought seducing an ex-wife might be an exciting game.

She returned to Elmhurst, driving above the safety limit. She had a groom saddle a horse and took some of her anger out in a hard exercise ride.

Late that afternoon, she was called to the telephone. A beautiful modulated female voice with a slight, intriguing accent spoke to her. "Miss Nikki Cameron?"

"Yes."

"This is Gina Anotia speaking. Perhaps you know of me?"

Nikki's mouth worked several times before she could make a sound come out. "Yes...yes, of course." The telephone lines hung icicles.

"I've heard a great deal about you, of course. You're the famous lady jockey."

Also the ex-wife of your current boyfriend, but what has that got to do with anything?

"What can I do for you?" Nikki asked in frigid tones.

"I want very much to meet you. I have something I must talk with you about. Could we possibly have dinner this evening?"

"I can't imagine what we'd have to talk about."

"It concerns Jacques Trenchard."

Again a rigid silence. Nikki's mind was in a tailspin. "What about Jacques?"

"It's really too personal and delicate to discuss on the telephone. If we could have a quiet dinner together..."

A world-famous actress and lady jockey having a quiet, private dinner? "How do you propose to do that?"

"I thought perhaps your lovely little country club. I spoke with the manager. He has some private rooms for just such occasions. He assures me we would not be disturbed."

"What time?"

"Could I meet you there at seven-thirty?"

"I guess so...."

Nikki hung up, stared at the phone and said, "Damn! Now why did I do that?" The last thing she wanted was to come face to face with Jacques' inamorata. What had possessed her to agree to such a meeting?

For the same unexplained reason, she spent extra time dressing, arranging her hair and applying makeup. Maybe, she thought, it was a woman's way of putting on boxing gloves.

Driving to the country club, she wondered why she should feel any animosity toward Gina Anotia. It was Jacques who filled her with murderous thoughts.

At the club, the manager directed her to one of the small, tastefully decorated private dining rooms. The actress was already there, seated on a couch. She rose with a flurry of jewels and furs, giving Nikki one of the dazzling smiles that entranced movie fans the world over.

"Why, you're lovely, Nikki," the Italian woman exclaimed. "So slim and feminine. Somehow I expected a lady jockey to be a rather masculine type of woman."

"Jockeys have to keep their weight down."

"Still, you must be wiry and in top physical condition to control a powerful thoroughbred." Again the actress's dazzling smile.

I bet she's rehearsed that so many times she switches it off and on like a light bulb, Nikki thought. She was not misled by the other woman's surface friendliness. Her green eyes were those of a combatant sizing up an opponent before going for the jugular.

However, Nikki had to admit she was gorgeous. With her flaming red hair, flashing green eyes and voluptuous figure, it was small wonder she was one of the most sought-after women in the world. Small wonder Jacques had chosen her.

A momentary picture flashed across Nikki's mind, the painful, wrenching vision of Gina's lush, naked body cradled in Jacques's arms. Something like a sharp knife stabbed through Nikki's stomach.

A waiter appeared.

"Shall we have cocktails before dinner?" Gina asked.

Nikki nodded. "Scotch with a splash," she told the waiter, who was staring at Gina.

"Ah, a man's drink," the actress said with a laugh.

"Not necessarily. I just don't see the point in spoiling good liquor with a lot of water."

"I see. Well, I'll have a martini. Very dry, please."

Very revealing, Nikki thought. Dry martini, a proper drink for a refined, sophisticated, cosmopolitan jetsetter. Scotch for the competing lady jockey.

"Please, can we sit and talk?"

Nikki nodded. She marveled at people who spoke like that. Each word was a musical note.

"Now then, Nikki," Gina Anotia said when they were seated on the couch with their drinks, "I'll tell you my reason for wanting to have this little chat with you. I'll come right to the point. It appears we are rivals, you and I."

"Rivals? Why, are you going to ride a horse in the Derby?"

Gina threw back her head, and this time her laughter actually sounded genuine. "How delightful you are. I can see why Jacques found you charming. No, I'm sure you know what I mean. We're rivals for the same man.''

"No we're not."

Gina looked surprised. For a fraction of a second her impeccable poise was derailed. ''Why do you say that?''

''If you're talking about Jacques Trenchard, I'm no rival. I despise the man. I want nothing to do with him.''

''Hmmm.'' Again the penetrating green-eyed gaze. ''I'd feel more reassured if you hadn't spoken with such passion. When a woman hates a man with such fervor, she could be covering up feelings just as strong in the other direction. Love and hate are very closely related, I believe.''

Her words caught Nikki off guard, making her uncomfortable. ''Ridiculous,'' she muttered. ''Look, Miss Anotia—''

''Gina, please.''

''Okay, Gina. Yes, I married Jacques six years ago when I was a starry-eyed teenager. It was a hasty marriage that ended as fast as it started. Why are you so concerned about me now?''

''Because Jacques has come here to the States. Because he bought a property next to yours. Because I think he wants to marry you.''

''He told you that?'' Nikki gasped.

''Yes. Do you know why?''

''Why he wants to marry me? Well, hardly because he loves me.''

''You're very perceptive. I'm glad for you. Obviously he broke your heart once, when you were young and idealistic. There's no point in allowing it to happen again. Nikki, I am going to be extremely frank with you. My cards on the table, as you Americans say. My motives? Selfish, yes. I'm not here out of altruistic reasons to keep you from being hurt. I'm fighting for the man I want for myself. It's true that Jacques wants to marry you. That has been part of his plan since he moved here. You see, Jacques loves me. We are two of a kind—citizens of the world. We travel in international circles. We speak the same social language, have the same friends. We have much in common. There is one very sad thing that keeps our relationship from being perfect. I can never have children. To a Frenchman like Jacques, with his strong sense of family tradition, having children—having an heir—is extremely important. Even more important than marrying me is having that son—your son. He is quite ready to marry you and then go through the legal process of adoption or whatever is necessary to make your Johnny his legal son. But that will not end our relationship—his and mine. I will continue to be his mistress. I'm willing to settle for that if it's the only way I can have him. You will become his official wife, the mistress of his estate in France. Perhaps you will bear him more children. But you will find that he must be away often for extended periods of time on 'business' trips. Those are the times he will be with me in Rome or London or Lisbon.''

Nikki sipped her drink. ''If you think you're surprising me with all this, you're mistaken. I had thought when he proposed that he might be doing it to get custody of Johnny.''

"I'm sorry, Nikki. Things like this can be painful. I hope you're not still in love with him. That would make it harder for you."

Gina reached for Nikki's hand, gave it a squeeze. Was it a gesture of genuine feeling? Nikki wasn't sure. A woman like Gina Anotia played so many roles, was she ever able to truly play herself?

In spite of all that, she found herself liking the actress. Nikki had come with a chip on her shoulder, but it was gone. Phony though she might be in many ways, Gina was able to convey a sense of warmth and charm that was disarming. And Nikki thought that she had no reason to feel animosity toward the other woman. If anything, she felt sorry for her. She was obviously in love with Jacques and frightened, afraid of losing him.

Nikki said, "Well, you don't have to worry. I am definitely not going to marry Jacques."

A look of relief filled Gina's eyes. "That makes me very happy. I told you I would be willing to settle for being his mistress if that's the only way I could have him, but of course I want more than that. I feel sure that if he becomes resigned to the fact that you will never marry him, then eventually he will marry me."

Nikki nodded. "That's fine with me. Now if you don't mind, I'm going to skip that dinner invitation. I'm really not hungry. Thanks for the drink. I'm going home and get some rest. I have some important races to win."

As she started to leave, she turned. "Maybe you can do something for me."

"I'll certainly try."

"I don't know if you're aware of this, but the property Jacques bought, Crestland, was my home. It was in my mother's family for generations ever since it was built. My grandfather lost it through some unfortunate circumstances. I want it back. If I win the Derby this year, I'll be in a position to make a substantial offer. I'd appreciate it if you could use your influence with Jacques to get him to sell it to me."

Gina gave one of her flashing smiles, "Yes. That would be fine. I'll do what I can to help you. You'd get what you want—your property back. And I'd get what I want—Jacques Trenchard. Then we'll both be happy."

"Of course."

With a great effort, Nikki was able to hold the tears back until she was out of the room.

Chapter Thirteen

Orlis Washington was quietly furious as he led Banshee from the winner's circle at Keeneland.

The grandstand, packed for the Blue Grass Stakes, was still pouring oceans of sound over the infield. Joyful bettors were streaming toward the pay windows to receive their two-to-one win on Banshee while the disconsolate threw down pari-mutuel tickets, singly or by the handful. A tout searched for a face whose owner he'd confidentially assured that Banshee was a sure thing, and a stooper in a threadbare, sleep-rumpled suit that suggested far better days was bent down and picking up thrown-away tickets in case some incensed on-the-nose loser had inadvertently cast aside in a bundle of tickets a show horse.

Breathless from the heady excitement of a first-place win and the trophy presentation, her Cameron silks stained from flying bits of track dirt, Nikki caught up with Orlis as he blanketed Banshee and started the big stallion on his cooling walk. The thoroughbred was still uptight, twitching, skittish but responding to the familiar kind and steady old hand on his halter rein.

Orlis looked straight ahead as Nikki fell in beside him.

"You old devil." Her Irish temper was beginning to rise. "What's eating you?"

"Who said anything's eating me?"

"Nobody has to. I know you. I had to practically run to catch up to you. Why aren't you speaking to me? What's stuck in your craw?"

Clop-clop-cloppety-clop. Banshee was cooling, settling down.

"You," Orlis finally said. "You're stuck like a chicken bone."

"Why, you…!" Nikki's hands balled into angry fists. She had to take a double step to catch up. "You've got a lot of nerve. Where do you get off acting like this? Listen, this was the Blue Grass. You understand? The Blue Grass Stakes. Stable, riders, owners, breeders— they dream about a Blue Grass win. And I won! I won, didn't I? Didn't I, Orlis?"

He shrugged. "It was a camera finish. You won by a nose whisker."

"A win's a win!" she cried furiously.

"Who are you mad at? Me or yourself?"

"What is that supposed to mean?"

"Now, Miss Nikki, you know better than saying that stuff about a win's a win. Banshee could have got by with just a camera finish by a whisker win today with any one of a dozen top jockeys on his back. He's never been better and as prime as the field was, it was just a foretaste of what'll be at the starting gate come Derby day."

"So?"

"I said it the first day of training after Gulfstream. I told you then and you just don't listen. You haven't faced it, Nikki."

"There's nothing to face!"

"Oh, there isn't?" Rhythmically moving, glancing up at Banshee's bobbing head, Orlis said, "You hear that, horse? Bad news, horse. For you and me and the lot of us. She's so blinded by her defenses that she doesn't know any longer. She hasn't had the guts to face it head-on and rise above it. Now she's convinced herself that it's not there, has never really been there. Isn't it amazing, horse, the way humans go around fooling themselves?"

Pacing him, looking straight ahead, distant shady oaks began to blur as Nikki felt tears quietly filling her eyes.

"How did you know, Orlis?"

"I've suspected from the results of several of your comeback races, Nikki, in spite of what the sportswriters have been saying. Like you, I didn't want to face it, either. But today, I had to. On that final turn, you were about two-hundredths of a second hesitant in shooting the gap. You rode a great race right up to then, nearly a perfect race, but from the final turn it was just another

performance by an average jock. Nothing great anymore. And that two-hundredth part of a clock tick almost cost us the race. Banshee deserves that fraction of
a second extra you were always able to give him, not the
other way around."

She sighed. "I knew when it happened, Orlis. But I
won, and I just refused to believe it had happened. I've
fought a hard fight to block it out every time it happened, thinking maybe it would just go away—that
flicker of the horrible instant from Gulfstream."

"Reminds me of a cousin I once had," Orlis said.
"He had a carbuncle in a mighty embarrassing location. It didn't hurt when he was up moving around,
chopping kindling, chewing the fat with a neighbor at
the gate post. He managed not to think about that carbuncle at all until he sat down at the dinner table."

"Orlis, what am I going to do?"

The trainer rubbed his jaw thoughtfully. "Maybe
you've already done it. You've finally faced the fact that
it's there. It may go away, and then again it may not. It
sure isn't going to be in any hurry taking its departure.
You're not going to expect it, want it, or encourage it.
But knowing it's there is like having a little sprain left in
an ankle. You jump from so high. You can cushion the
ankle in advance for the drop through space. You're not
going to let the ankle keep you from jumping, but you
won't pretend that it's as sound as the other, either. And
one day you'll jump and not have a twitch in the ankle
to deal with."

"I know...I know...."

"Then you be chastised twice, girl! All this time
you've been jumping and pretending that the ankle

won't twitch, and when it did, you had to stop for the fractional part of a second to deal with the twitch. You have to start facing the possibility right up front when the bell is about to clang at the starting gate. You accept it and live with it and refuse to let it throw you. Then you're ready for it when it happens—and on a far turn you can go and shoot the gap as only a really great jockey can.''

They paced in silence, remote from the other horses and grooms. "Well," Nikki said with a quiet smile, "I guess you ought to thank me, Orlis."

"For what?"

"Giving you a chance to get the slow burn off your chest."

"What's a friend for if you can't spout off once in a while?"

"A friend, a real and true friend, is a rare treasure, Orlis."

"Then we're still friends?"

"Good grief! What a dumb question to come from a cunning old lifetime friend." Then she gave Banshee a loving pat and said, "Well, you take good care of my big baby here and I'm off to the showers."

The anticipated luxury of getting out of dirty racing silks was delayed when a small cadre of reporters and photographers descended on her as she neared the jockeys' quarters.

"There she is!"

She recognized some of the faces. A portable camera carried by a local TV sportscaster was staring at her. A reporter from the Louisville paper was there, as was a stringer who wrote for one of the national racing sheets. She had an easy smile for all of them.

"Please, guys, one at a time," she said, holding up a pleading hand as she was bombarded with questions. "Actually I haven't much to say about the race. It's the horse that does the running, you know. As for myself, I can't improve on the usual platitudes: tight race...happy to have won...yes, we're looking forward to the Derby."

"And on to the Triple Crown, Nikki?"

It was a breath-catching thought, one she'd not quite dared to entertain. She laughed. "If you guys expect to goad me into a quote that'll get a rise from the opposition ranks and give you a story, sorry. One race at a time. You have to win at Churchill Downs before you can even think of the other two jewels in the Triple Crown—Belmont, the Preakness."

"Then you're predicting a Derby win?"

Nikki glanced at the speaker, a stranger. "I'm not predicting anything. You're a sly bunch of foxes, but you'd better not pin a quote like that on me."

"You feel that they're just three more races on the card?" the reporter persisted. Nikki new the story heading he was after: *Top Female Jockey Downgrades Triple Crown.*

Little wonder, Nikki thought grimly, that a politician learns how to talk much and say little during a press conference.

"No race," she said, choosing her words carefully, "is just another on the card. The Triple is a card unto itself, each a Super Bowl of competing champions, the greatest challenge of any World Series in the world of sports.''

"In your opinion, then, the other sports—professional football, baseball, basketball—don't begin to compare?''

The fellow simply wouldn't give up, trying to put words in her mouth, determined to get a story angle— any angle. *Glamorous Lady Jock Pooh-Poohs Male-Dominated Sports.*

Nikki concluded that he had to be from one of the more lurid tabloids.

A reporter she knew broke in. "The least intelligent among us knows where Nikki Cameron stands. She's a champion. As a human being, jockey, wherever she goes, whatever she does, she's a champion. Nikki, is it true that Banshee has shaded Derby time once on the Elmhurst training track?''

With her eyes, Nikki thanked him for his attitude, but her smile was careful. "I'm not always at the training track. I don't know how that rumor got started. I'll take it back to Elmhurst. Now, please, fellows. You've got your picture with me at the worst. How about a chance to wash a small part of the track off my face?''

Easily, pleasantly, she resumed her way, waving a hand in a no-no as they continued to hurl questions. Nikki was well attuned to the importance of good public relations with the media. It was part of the public, professional life she had chosen.

Then, nearing the doorway that would let her enter the building where she could shower, she froze in her tracks as if on the edge of a precipice. All the noise and activity of Keeneland dissolved into nothingness.

"Hello, Nikki," Jacques said.

His presence flowed over her. Looking up at him, she almost took a step backward. She wanted her lips to stop their unbidden quivering and curl up in icy disdain. She wanted her eyes to despise him, but her gaze only floundered.

"Nikki..."

"I'm in a hurry," she said curtly. "Excuse me." She made a movement to slide past him. His hands caught her elbows.

"Will you please," she said in a voice that was unsteady, "take your hands off me."

"I will if you'll let me talk to you for a minute. What's gotten into you? You suddenly act as if I have the plague."

"That's a good description. Now go away before you give it to me."

He looked perplexed, angry. "You're not even civil."

"I'm not trying to be."

"I don't understand. Have I said something—done something?"

"Oh, you've done a lot. But that's not important. I just don't want to talk to you, Jacques. Can I make it any clearer?"

"Yes, you can make it a lot clearer." Now he was angry. "We had a perfectly delightful time together in New Orleans. You kissed me with a great deal of passion. If you recall, I proposed marriage. You promised to think it over. Now you're behaving as if I insulted you."

"Well, that's a pretty good description of what you did—or what you're trying to do."

He shook his head, looking more bewildered. "Either the race today scrambled your brains or I'm missing something. I believe you owe me an explanation and I'm going to get it."

"Is that a threat?" she asked, her eyes flashing.

"Perhaps. Why won't you tell me why you're so angry?"

"Maybe because my eyes have been opened to your motives, Jacques Trenchard."

They were beginning to draw curious stares. Lowering his voice, Jacques said, "This is no place to have a private conversation. Meet me for dinner after you get cleaned up so we can have a halfway intelligent discussion. Surely you owe me that much."

Yes, she admitted she did. No matter how angry she was, she could not forget that she owed him a tremendous debt, one she could never repay. Jacques' heroism had saved the lives of both Orlis and Banshee the night of that dreadful fire at Elmhurst. He had risked his life without hesitation. She would always admire him for that. The least she could do now was contain her anger enough to be civil. Reluctantly, she agreed. "All right." She sighed. "Where shall we meet?"

"I'll make a reservation at Hake's Also Ran."

"Very well. I'll meet you there."

Hake was a huge, ever-smiling and gregarious man who claimed he'd opened his restaurant in order to get a good meal five times a day. The menu was southern, the taste was gourmet. A natural stone-and-tile farmhouse a short distance out of Paris Pike had been converted to Hake's specifications. A long, narrow room, once the sun parlor, was a quietly busy bar done in dark

woods and brass specializing in, not surprisingly, ju-
leps and planter's punch. The dining room contained a
soothing aura of intimate privacy, plush carpeting, deep
maroon wall coverings and linen on the tables in
matching tones. The captain's chairs were cushioned
leather. Customers pulling up at the veranda on a soft
summer evening for valet parking immediately got an
appetizing whiff of aromas from the kitchen that had
elevated southern cooking to a fine art.

As Nikki entered the foyer, which was lit by a brass-
and-crystal chandelier, Hake was there to extend his
usual hearty greeting.

"Ah, we have a celebrity with us tonight. Nikki
Cameron! How good of you to add a rare touch of love-
liness to the old farmhouse!"

Nikki knew he was sincere. Hake loved everybody.
His rotund figure was dressed in a tentlike tuxedo. His
round head was as bald as an egg and matched the
pinkness of his cheeks. "How is everyone at
Elmhurst?"

"Just fine."

"Elvira?"

"Spunky as ever. She'll outlive us all. And you're
looking super, Hake."

"It's the good cooking. Hey, you and Banshee...absolutely superb out there today. Wish I'd had
more than a measly thousand on the nose."

He was escorting her along a softly lighted hallway,
opening a door to a dining room that had once been a
study. At the door stood a smiling waiter shadowed by
a busboy. He took over, bowing a welcome and hold-

ing a chair for Nikki at the table where Jacques had risen.

As usual she'd brought the most basic wardrobe with her to the track. It had included slacks, blouses, two pairs of shoes, necessary underthings, skirt, jacket, jeans and sweat shirt. A single item of dressy apparel was always tossed in should she have to attend a function relevant to her profession. In this instance she had included a dress of midnight black that caught blue overtones when she turned or moved. Her jewelry was artfully simple beaten Mexican silver-and-turquoise earrings and chain necklace.

Jacques' eyes swept over her. "Quite a transformation from the riding silks. You're lovely, Nikki."

"Cut the compliments, Jacques. I'm here for two reasons. I haven't eaten all day, so I'm starved. The other is to tell you off for once and all and get you to stop bothering me."

Again the dark anger glowed in Jacques' eyes, but he contained it. "A before-dinner cocktail?" he asked coldly.

"Are you serious? As empty and hungry as I am? I'd fall flat on my face."

"Then we'll order dinner right away." Jacques and the waiter discussed the menu briefly. The barbecue was always from stone-lined earthen pits, a full twelve hours in slow, careful preparation. A prime side of beef was especially good tonight, said the waiter.

After the waiter jotted down the order and went away, Nikki glanced about the room. Hake never sought the extra dollar by crowding in tables. Each dining room preserved for each table its own private space. Here she and Jacques could converse freely.

"Now," Jacques said, "perhaps you will enlighten me as to the reason for this sudden vicious mood you are in?"

Nikki looked at him sullenly. "You're a first-class rat, you know that, Jacques Trenchard?"

"Oh, I am? And why is that?"

"Why is that? Because while you were wining and dining me at Antoine's and wooing me with flowers and all that sweet talk about wanting to marry me again, your girlfriend was on her way over to shack up with you."

He raised an eyebrow, looking baffled. "Are you talking about Gina Anotia?"

"Who else? Don't try to lie and say she's not staying at Crestland."

The expression of anger in Jacques' eyes faded into one of amusement. "Now I get it." He actually chuckled, which further infuriated Nikki. "The old green monster has you in its grip. You're burning with jealousy. That's a very good sign, my dear Nikki. It proves that you do care about me and you will marry me again."

"It proves you are a totally unprincipled, two-faced scoundrel and I wouldn't remarry you if you were the last man on the face of the earth."

"It's true Gina is a house guest at Crestland. I don't deny it. We have a constant flow of friends from the continent as house guests. My doors are always open to my friends. To be frank, half the time I'm not sure who is there. I didn't know until this afternoon that Gina had flown in for a visit between films. I've been in New York all week.''

"I don't believe you."

"But it's true. Gina is not my mistress, despite all the gossip in the scandal tabloids. She's a friend, no more."

"You want to bet she isn't in love with you?"

"Perhaps she is," he said with a shrug. "So are a number of women."

"What an ego!" Nikki exploded.

Jacques merely chuckled. "I'm only being realistic, Nikki. I have considerable wealth. I'm single. That alone would be enough to qualify me as fair game even if I looked like the hunchback of Notre Dame."

"Well, that's your side of the story. Gina told me that you want to marry me only because of Johnny."

He looked surprised. "She spoke with you?"

"Yes. And I believe her."

"It didn't occur to you she might be making all that up to turn you against me?"

"No, because I had suspected from the beginning that's what your real motive was in wanting to remarry me. You don't care anything about me. It's your son you want."

He shook his head slowly. "What do I have to do to convince you? It's all so very simple. Why do you muddy everything up with your doubts? Nikki, please marry me again."

"And return to France."

"Yes, as a family. Of course we'll keep Crestland, too. You will be a full-time wife and mother."

"In charge of Château Trenchard."

"What's so bad about that?"

"And you'd expect me to give up racing."

"Yes. But you don't have to give up horses. Horses are a part of my life, too. What's so terrible about membership in a hunt club, organizing horse shows?"

"Seeing my picture in a riding habit and my name on the social pages! You see, nothing has changed. As your wife, you expect me to be an extension of Jacques Trenchard's ego. I'm a living, breathing individual, Jacques, a person in my own right, with my own career, my own goals. You refused to accept me on those terms the first time. It's the same now. Nothing has changed."

"Perhaps I know what's best for you. We all know you came very close to getting killed at Gulfstream. The next time you may not be so lucky. I suspect that deep in your subconscious you'd like to hang up the jockeys silks. That accident left its emotional scar. I know a few things about horses myself, you'll have to admit. I wasn't a two-dollar player watching the race today. Banshee was in top form. He should have won by a full length...."

Orlis had lectured her about that and now this pride-stinging verdict from Jacques. It was too much, just too much!

She retorted furiously, "I'm as good as I ever was!"

"Perhaps." His eyes narrowed, grew thoughtful. Then he said, "Suppose I put my marriage proposal in terms that are dearest to your heart. My horse, Le Cheval, and Banshee will both be in the Derby. I know how much you want Crestland. If you win, I will give you the deed to the estate, give up trying to marry you and return to France. But if you lose, you will hang up

the silks and marry me. How is that for a wager, my
lady jockey? Do you really think you're good enough
to take on that kind of bet?''

They faced each other in the candlelight during a taut
silence. High rollers, the both of us, she thought. All or
nothing. It's the only kind of language we seem able to
speak.

She chewed her lip, torn with the sweeping implication of his wager.

"You see," he said quietly, "you do know that the
Gulfstream accident—"

"Did nothing to me!" she retorted, her pride stung.
"All right, Jacques Trenchard. I accept your wager!"

Chapter Fourteen

Among Nikki's earliest memories was the excitement of Derby Week, the exuberant annual event for which Louisville prepares far in advance. The festival smacked of Mardi Gras, Tournament of Roses, Orange Festival added to the flavor of an old-time state fair revved to staggering proportions.

America experienced nothing quite like the ushering in of the spring-summer meets at Churchill Downs. As the calendar melted April into May, the busy modern metropolis of three hundred thousand people, which cut its jagged, sprawling skyline along a long curve in the mighty Ohio River, let its hair down for the week-long winging that had something for everyone.

The temporary population explosion comes from all points of the compass. The springtime ritual was a

conclave of the thoroughbred world, from the shoe-
string breeder in his threadbare, carefully pressed
Brooks Brothers suit to the Syrian who'd had his
custom-made Mercedes flown over to whisk him about
the sights. A dirt farmer loaded his family in their rattling pickup truck and headed for Louisville. A high-
level politician planned his break from Washington so
he could make the event. Socialite friends from London and New York anticipated Derby Week over a
penthouse luncheon. The Hollywood star would bring
her personal hairdresser along in preparation for the
moment when twenty million people would catch her on
TV as the guest of the governor at the Downs. The
cream of sportswriters, columnists and television journalists would arrive and set up shop.

Private homes hummed the note of parties. Children
had ice cream, favors and games on lawns. Grownups
gathered about swimming pools and barbecue grills.
There were black-tie events at mansions. Caterers set
out food in invitation-only hotel suites, where the minimum purchase of poker chips wᶜs twenty-five thousand dollars.

The public scene was a montage of unceasing festiv-
ities: hot-air balloon races, official receptions, Porsche
drivers competing at one location and high-perform-
ance go-carts in a grand prix of their own at another.
There were floats and bands in street parades, country-
western hoedowns, regattas on the river, the race between giant Mississippi paddle wheelers, horse shows
and displays of antique automobiles, tea dances for
senior citizens and marathon runs open to all, tours of
historic homes and sites, plain fun events such as the

Run for the Rose, wherein waiters and waitresses from area restaurants raced for prizes through an obstacle course while holding trays of wine-filled glasses. There were concerts of every variety from Dixieland to rock.

And it was all like a giant lens pinpointing those two minutes facing horses and riders in the starting gate for the event at the Downs known as the Kentucky Derby.

Try as she might, Nikki couldn't quite grasp a sense of reality from the final hours and minutes when post time came rushing to meet her. The butterflies in her stomach left little room for food. Not that she would allow herself to eat much anyway, needing to measure her weight in terms of ounces. She was up at dawn looking at the sky before it was fully revealed outside her hotel window. The night had brought a springtime shower. She read signs of a clear, sunny day. So far, so good. That meant a perfect track for Banshee.

She moved through the unreal space and time to the roar of a hundred and fifty thousand spectators washing over her and she thought, Well, here I am. At the Downs, where the formal gardens are the loveliest on earth and the mind-boggling grandstand has the two fragile-looking spires beside its gables and...Oh, Lord! I wish I were a trainer out there in the vastness of the stables hearing pigeons fussing in the rafters while I checked on a horse instead of a rider who has the responsibility of winning or losing the race.

"I'm going to be a jockey someday myself," a small voice ventured shyly at Nikki's elbow.

Nikki turned with a slightly startled look from her locker. Standing just on the other side of the wooden bench fronting the lockers was a slender teenage girl with olive skin and black hair that curled slightly at its short tips. She was the valet girl who'd seen to Nikki's work clothes—the black boots with mirror shine, the pants, the silk in the black-and-white slashings of Cameron colors.

"You don't look crazy." Nikki laughed.

"Oh, but it isn't crazy at all. If you can make it all the way to the big one—well, you proved a woman can do it. I've—I've got a scrapbook of clippings about you...."

In the act of peeling off the slipover top of her street wear, Nikki halted for an instant. Momentarily she recalled her own scrapbook, started long ago. In a flash, she saw it all, the rodeos, the rusty old van, the quarter horse outlaw tracks, the hard, gruelling training, the aching body, the heartbreak of losing, the intoxication of winning, the determination, the joy, the fear. All of it was in the faded pages of her own scrapbook—all of it leading up to this moment, today.

"I mean," the girl said, coloring faintly, "you won't be by yourself out there today. I don't mean just me. I don't matter that much. But people everywhere. You're kind of a symbol. Look, let me get you something. Please?"

Nikki smiled at her eagerness. The girl was hardly more than a child. But then, Nikki thought, so had she been when she started on this tough, demanding road to today. "Okay," she said. "A small orange juice. No ice, but very cold."

The girl skipped off happily and Nikki sank down on the bench for a moment, feeling as if the girl had added another ten pounds to her slender shoulders. She drew a breath and rose to continue dressing.

The locker-room girl came back carrying a large Styrofoam cup filled to the brim. Disrobed to her underthings—slender, svelte, smooth as satin—Nikki thanked her. She took a sip, then set the drink on the bench and started wriggling into her pants. "What if I should lose today?"

"Oh, we'd all love you just the same for the person you are."

Nikki's eyes stung; for some unfathomable reason she found herself thinking of Jacques with a sudden hurting stab. How ironic it was. To win she must lose. To lose she must win. If the race was hers, so was Crestland, but Jacques would bow out of her life forever. If she lost, she lost Crestland, and she would have to marry Jacques or welsh on her bet. But what kind of a marriage would that be? No love. She would just be the trophy he had captured at the Downs. A marriage under those circumstances wouldn't last any longer than it had the first disastrous time.

She swam onward through the stark clarity of the unreal day. It became a mixed blur, the weigh-in, carrying her tack. The barns. The pat and grin for Banshee. Sunlight on her face.

Colby was standing there before her at the barn while the tidal waves of grandstand noise seemed far away.

"I guess—" her father grinned somewhat self-consciously "—I'm here because it's standard ritual for a trainer to give those last minute instructions to a jockey. Nothing has happened to suggest a last minute change of tactics, Nikki. About all I can say is Godspeed. We've analyzed every horse and rider in this race, and unless one of them has developed an overnight quirk, we know them almost as well as they know themselves. We've drawn number three post position. The track, after the light shower last night followed by all the sun today, offers Banshee his favorite running surface."

Nikki knew. Fortune had smiled. Everything seemed right. If she didn't ride a winning race today, she had nothing to blame but herself.

"Walleyed Wally and Le Cheval are our two biggest concerns," her father said, "although you're up against a whole field of potential record breakers. Sappington, Walleye's jockey, will be content to lay back, third or fourth, maneuvering for position as far as the final turn; then he'll let the chestnut run like a sprinter through the final three furlongs. Le Cheval is something else. Could be the horse we know least. Rooster Malone will be in Le Cheval's saddle as he was at Keeneland, where he had a chance to learn your riding firsthand. He'll be out to make up for that loss to you, Nikki, and the little guy can lick five times his weight in a barroom brawl. He's just plain mean. Also, my instincts warn me about Le Cheval's owner. I keep having this hunch that Jacques hasn't fully taken the wraps off his horse, letting him out just enough to get him here today, but holding back that extra hundredth of a second he's capable of running."

Colby lapsed into silence. Their eyes met in a moment of silent communication. He gave her hand a brief squeeze, turned and was gone.

Nikki had never felt more alone.

The routine might have been a prelude to any race. The paddock walk. The post parade. The announcer's voice booming introductions to each horse on a loud-speaker that could make itself heard above the tide of noise from thousands of throats. She felt Banshee's supple power tightening and quivering beneath her. She wondered if the big stallion was as anxious and dry-throated as she.

There was the brief warm-up...and how incredibly long and empty the track appeared! Then they were at the starting gate at last, Banshee entering with nervous tossings of his head.

Goggles down. She made a fractional shift of foot in the left stirrup. She felt her weight in perfect balance. Her reins were in delicately communicating hands.

The sense of suspense became acute, unbearable as a hush swept over the grandstand and thousands of hearts expectantly strained for the start.

Nikki was ready, primed. This time she let it happen, the lightning flicker behind her eyes of the moment she'd carried with her since that day at Gulfstream. This time she didn't react with an instant spinning away of her mind to avoid it; not this time. She didn't shut it out and pretend a denial. She faced the black monster straight on. Was she afraid? Could it happen again? Today? Yes.

Then she thought, The worst thing that could happen to me is that I'd get killed. That kind of resignation had a strangely calming effect.

Then that special hair-trigger mechanism in Banshee suddenly communicated itself to her. The stallion had a weirdly thoroughbred antenna that seemed to detect the pressure of the starter's thumb on the button of the bell.

She and the big horse were poised as one entity, a volatile package about to explode.

"They're off!"

The familiar boom from the loudspeaker concurred with the clang of the bell and the swell of sound from the crowd.

It was like a cannonade with twenty horses as projectiles. Banshee was out of the chute smoothly. Le Cheval, coming from fifth post position, was nose to nose. Past the grandstand, Walleyed Wally seemed content to run fourth as the field began to string out and define itself. Frank's Folly stretched out his early lead; his single hope was to stay there with enough left for the final two furlongs.

Nikki let Banshee ease up to third, keeping the first turn tight while Sappington on Walleye cursed himself for permitting the slight outer drift.

On his feet, watching from his clubhouse box, Jacques kept his binoculars zeroed in on Nikki. So far he had never witnessed a better ride, and he'd seen the best that England, France, Ireland and America had to offer. He was witnessing a rare talent using itself, fulfilling itself, rewarding in full measure the milieu wherein it functioned.

A tender pride, bitterly sweet, stung his eyes. And with it came a stab of self-recrimination. Why had he only added to the burdens testing her spirit and courage? Why, from the accident at Gulfstream to this moment, had he let her battle it all alone, the psychological Gulfstream scar that would have kept a lesser woman from being out there at this moment pitting herself against a field of champions? Selfishly, he knew, he had hoped she would lose the battle, give up her dangerous career and accept the life he'd offered. But what could he offer?

All she wanted for her modest self had always been within her reach. She had clearly and courageously set about getting money for that single extra she needed— Crestland. He could offer her position, but who could speak to her of position? In her own right she was a top name in her chosen profession. Her father was nationally known and respected in his field. Nikki knew tycoons, movie stars, famous sports journalists, high-echelon politicians who'd shared her company at the Elmhurst dinner table. She would be welcomed in the mansion of an Arab sheikh or the castle of a Scottish clan. She had friends from stable muckers to an ex-governor. She measured them all with the same yardstick. In her own right, she was as much an internationally known personality as was he.

No, there was only one thing anyone could offer Nikki Cameron, and that was love.

His straining eyes felt scorched. He gasped. The field glasses jammed harder against his eye sockets, watching as Nikki and Rooster Malone neared the three-eighths pole, going into the far turn. The jockey hadn't missed that single weakness Nikki had revealed at Keeneland two weeks ago. It figured in his strategy. Avoid a disqualifying bump, but at the right instant, move on her. She'd hesitate. Cut her off, then fight it out with the remaining leaders on the homestretch for the win. Damn him! Jacques swore. He had specifically ordered his trainer not to let that mean little jockey of his use that kind of tactic. He wanted to win, yes, but not by exploiting Nikki's weakness.

On Banshee, Nikki saw it coming, caught a flash of the tight-lipped grimace on the face of Rooster Malone, felt the crowding, the nearness of the rail. The Gulfstream situation all over again. Her hands became icy clamps on the reins. But this time, she didn't blank it out of her mind, allowing her subconscious reflexes to control her actions, communicating that split-second hesitation to Banshee. This time she faced the monster head-on, spit in his eye and yelled in Banshee's ear, "Run, you big, powerful devil! Run!"

And Banshee ran with all his sinew and muscle and great, heroic heart and she flashed through the gap. Not a single hundredth of a second was lost in faltering uncertainty. Now, nearing the quarter pole, the homestretch almost in sight, it was Le Cheval falling behind and Walleyed Wally coming up nose to nose to challenge Banshee in that last desperate sprint to the finish line.

She screamed, "Banshee, do it! Dig it out! You're great, Banshee! Great!"

She felt the response—the stretch of tendons already stretched beyond limit, the powerful lungs gasping, the great heart matching her own refusal to falter.

Frank's Folly tired at last, and his flank, rolling eyes and bobbing, streaming nose slipped behind the powerhouse called Banshee. Le Cheval was half a length behind now, his rider's face a mask of murderous fury.

Then it was Walleyed Wally making his final move, squeezing out the last ounce of reserve in the rush to the finish line. Banshee picked up the challenge and hurled it back. Nose to nose the two horses inched into the lead.

"Stretch, Banshee! Stretch!"

Nikki glimpsed Walleyed Walley's mane as Banshee stretched his flaring nostrils toward the wire.

She knew.

It was a photo finish. But she knew. She didn't need a photograph to tell her.

She was too experienced not to know.

Grandstand thunder filled the sunny day while she let Banshee slow from hard run to gallop to canter, to a sidestepping, head-tossing easing of tension that took them on around the track.

She was sobbing when eager hands carried her down from the saddle. A groom took the reins, but she ran to Banshee, holding on to his neck. "You tried, honey....Please don't feel bad...you tried so hard...."

Somewhere in the sea of faces, there was Orlis, his hand with awkward tenderness on her shoulder. "Don't you cry so, Nikki. You ran the best race of your life today. You licked that thing that's been eating you. That counts for something—"

"But we lost, Orlis," she sobbed. "We lost...."

"Inside you won. You licked what's been hurting you so badly ever since you were injured. That counts for something. That counts for a lot. I'm very proud of you—"

It was all mixed up, confused. The army of security guards holding back the crowds. The sportscasters, television cameras, speech by the governor. She hurt so much. Her body ached from the pounding of the track.

Her throat was filled with a suffocating lump. Her eyes burned from tears that kept streaming down her face.

She was finally escorted to the women's dressing room by a ring of uniformed security men. Somehow Colby got there ahead of her and was waiting at the doorway.

Nikki went blindly into his arms. He held her tight, soothing her hair. "I know, honey. I know."

"Daddy, I tried so hard...."

"I know you did, honey. We all know. Don't cry so. You did everything humanly possible. Banshee ran his heart out. It just wasn't in the cards, that's all."

"We had it won and then in that last fraction of a second..."

"It's what gives horse racing its suspense, those unpredictable upsets at the last second."

Then a fresh realization brought more bitter tears. She had lost more than a horse race today. She had lost Crestland.

"Dad, I'm going to take my shower now," she said wearily. "We'll talk some more later."

"Sure, you do that, honey." He moved away. Then, remembering something: "Oh, I almost forgot. Jacques gave this to me before the race. He said to hold on to it and give it to you after the race. Something about not wanting to distract you before the race."

He placed a thick white envelope in her hand. Numbly, she accepted it and went into the dressing room. She moved slowly to the wooden bench in front of the lockers and sat down. Weariness was engulfing her, the overwhelming letdown after the tension that had saturated her with adrenaline. Now came the reaction, the release, the depression.

She stared at the envelope, hardly having the energy to open it. Why would Jacques leave something like this for her?

Her fingers felt clumsy and inept as she tore open the envelope.

Inside was a legal document.

It was the deed to Crestland.

There was a letter:

Nikki, darling,

However the race turns out today, I want you to have this. I know how much Crestland means to you. It should belong to you. Perhaps in a small way it can make up for all the mistakes, for the heartache I have caused you. It is a token of how much I love you. If you win, it's yours anyway with my congratulations. If you lose, I certainly will not hold you to the ridiculous wager that you have to marry me. I will continue to hope one day you will marry me because I love you and I want you and me and our son to be a family, but not because of an impulsive wager.

I love you,
Jacques

For long moments, Nikki stared at the note. The tears came again, but now they were a gentle flow of emotion from an overflowing heart. "Jacques," she choked. "You sentimental fool. I didn't think you had it in you!"

She had showered and dressed when a message was delivered to her. It read, "Would you have a drink with me in the clubhouse? Jacques."

She shook her head, smiling crookedly. "Why does he always use those fancy cards with his embossed family crest in gold? I'd be as happy if he wrote the note on the back of an envelope."

When she arrived at the clubhouse, she found Jacques. But he wasn't alone. Nikki's spirits took a nosedive. At the table beside him was the lovely Gina Anotia.

Jacques quickly rose, drew a chair out for her. Gina gave her a cool nod.

"What a splendid race!" Jacques exclaimed. "Nikki, you were superb."

"Thank you, but not superb enough to win."

Jacques shrugged and waved his hand in a fatalistic gesture. *"C'est la vie."*

"Whatever that means," Nikki said.

"It means, 'That's life.'"

"It sure is. Look, I didn't know you had company. Maybe we can talk later—"

She started to rise, but Jacques put his hand on her arm, restraining her. "Gina was just leaving. She's on her way to Italy to start a new movie. But she has something to say to you first." He looked at the Italian star, his eyes stern. "Gina."

She fingered her cocktail glass, avoiding Nikki's eyes. "I...just wanted to tell you to forget what I said that day at the country club. Jacques has never been my lover." She looked at him with tears filling her eyes. "Though I wish he were."

She rose abruptly. "Good-bye. I have a plane to catch." She gave Jacques a last tear-filled look, then her high heels beat a rapid staccato across the floor.

"Well!" Nikki exclaimed, feeling somewhat embarrassed and unsure how to deal with the surprising development. "How did you get her to tell me that?"

"Twisted her arm a bit."

"How?"

He chuckled. "It's my money that's financing the next film she's going to do. I threatened to cancel the deal unless she told you the truth. Nikki, Gina has never meant anything to me. I'm not sure I actually mean all that much to her. It's her sense of drama, I think. I've been a challenge. Half the men in Europe have thrown themselves at her feet. One of them threatened to jump out of a ten-story window. It hurt her ego that I didn't fall for her charms."

"Why didn't you? She's gorgeous."

"Yes, she's very beautiful. But I happen to be in love with somebody else." His dark eyes reached deeply into Nikki, giving her a feeling of consternation.

She looked down at her hands that were nervously clenched in her lap. "Jacques, I don't know how to thank you for what you did. I mean about giving me Crestland. That—that was an awfully generous gesture."

"It wasn't just a gesture. You read my note?"

"Y-yes..."

She could no longer avoid his powerful dark eyes. They drew her gaze with hypnotic force. "I meant every word in that note, Nikki, my darling. I love you with all my heart. I've regretted many times the way our first marriage ended. It was the greatest mistake of my life to let you go. When I saw you again, I realized how empty those six years had been. I have met many women during those years all over the world, but none of them touched me here." He took her hand and placed it over his heart. "This is where you are, Nikki. Where you'll always be. No one else could take your place."

She swallowed hard. "Jacques, you speak so beautifully—your words are like poetry."

"Love is poetry, beautiful, fragile, touching the soul. Nikki...Nikki, please say you'll forgive me for my stupid mistakes. Say you'll give me another chance."

"But we'll have the same old fights over my career. You'll try to take over and run my life like a European husband and I'll rebel and then we'll say terrible things to each other and get another divorce—"

He held up his right hand. "I promise not to do that anymore. I've learned my lesson, Nikki. I saw it in your ride today. Being a jockey is not just something you do. It's what you are. It's your life. Perhaps your reason for being. I'll keep on hoping that one day you'll decide it's time to stop. But I swear I will never again make it an issue in our relationship."

Jacques suggested a European honeymoon. Nikki said, "No. We went that route once before. I want to go home for my honeymoon—home to Crestland."

Jacques carried her up the stairs on their wedding night and into their bedroom. Everything was so right about that. Many years ago her grandfather had carried his bride across this threshold, and his father before him.

Had they been in love as much as she was in love tonight? she wondered as her husband tenderly slipped her gown from her shoulder.

She smiled into his eyes, her bare arms around his neck. "Think we remember how to do this? It's been six years."

"I don't think we've forgotten." He smiled back.

Her eyes grew heavy-lidded, her breath deeper as his caresses warmed her body.

"Oh, how I've missed you," she whispered huskily. "We've got six years to make up."

"That will be a pleasure."

Their bodies were entwined. His arms were steel bands around her. She moaned, her eyes closed. She welcomed him, feeling so right to be a part of this wonderful, heroic man who was her husband now, loving him with her body and her heart, joined to him forever, wanting him to carry her to the heights of ecstasy, giving of herself competely, holding nothing back, surrendering, and glorying in the surrender, wanting him to possess her and reveling in the flame that he awoke deep inside her.

Later, as dawn lightened the window, she lay contentedly in his arms amidst the tangled bedclothing.

"Jacques," she murmured dreamily.

"Yes, my darling wife?"

"Y'know what?"

"What?"

"I have a feeling that next year I'm going to win the Derby."

He sighed. "I wouldn't be the least bit surprised."

The Silhouette Cameo Tote Bag Now available for just $6.99

Handsomely designed in blue and bright pink, its stylish good looks make the Cameo Tote Bag an attractive accessory. The Cameo Tote Bag is big and roomy (13″ square), with reinforced handles and a snap-shut top. You can buy the Cameo Tote Bag for $6.99, plus $1.50 for postage and handling.

Send your name and address with check or money order for $6.99 (plus $1.50 postage and handling), a total of $8.49 to:

**Silhouette Books
120 Brighton Road
P.O. Box 5084
Clifton, NJ 07015-5084
ATTN: Tote Bag**

SIL-T-1

The Silhouette Cameo Tote Bag can be purchased pre-paid only. No charges will be accepted. Please allow 4 to 6 weeks for delivery.

Arizona and N.Y. State Residents Please Add Sales Tax

Offer not available in Canada.

If you're ready for a more sensual, more provocative reading experience...

We'll send you 4 Silhouette Desire novels

FREE...

and without obligation

Then, we'll send you six more Silhouette Desire® novels to preview every month for 15 days with absolutely no obligation!

When you decide to keep them, you pay just $1.95 each ($2.25, in Canada), *with no shipping, handling, or additional charges of any kind!*

Silhouette Desire novels are not for everyone. They are written especially for the woman who wants a more satisfying, more deeply involving reading experience.

Silhouette Desire novels take you *beyond* the others and offer real-life drama and romance of successful women in charge of their lives. You'll share

Silhouette Special Edition

COMING NEXT MONTH

SUMMER DESSERTS—Nora Roberts
Blake Cocharan wanted the best, and Summer Lyndon was a dessert chef *extraordinaire*. She had all of the ingredients he was looking for, and a few he didn't expect.

HIGH RISK—Caitlin Cross
Paige Bannister had lived life from a safe distance until she met rodeo rider Casey Cavanaugh and found herself taking risks she had never thought she would dare.

THIS BUSINESS OF LOVE—Alida Walsh
Working alongside executive producer Steve Bronsky was a challenge that Cathy Arenson was willing to meet, but resisting his magnetic charm was more than a challenge—it was an impossibility.

A CLASS ACT—Kathleen Eagle
Rafe had always thought that Carly outclassed him, but when she was caught in a blizzard nothing mattered other than warming her by his fire…and in his arms.

A TIME AND A SEASON—Curtiss Ann Matlock
Two lovers were thrown together on a remote Oklahoma highway. Katie found Reno easy to love, but could she embrace life on his ranch as easily as she embraced him?

KISSES DON'T COUNT—Linda Shaw
Reuben North hadn't planned on becoming involved, but when Candice's old boyfriend threatened to take her child away, Reuben found himself comfortably donning his shining armor.

AVAILABLE NOW:

THE HEART'S YEARNING
Ginna Gray

STAR-CROSSED
Ruth Langan

A PERFECT VISION
Monica Barrie

MEMORIES OF THE HEART
Jean Kent

AUTUMN RECKONING
Maggi Charles

ODDS AGAINST TOMORROW
Patti Beckman